Stonechild

by

Kevin Albin

ISBN 9798667616313

The beginning ...

Six-year-old Molly Hargreaves let go of her father's hand and stepped onto the first, large, grey flagstone. Taking a small shuffle and a graceful skip, she reached the next one without stepping on the crack between the two. She was now that much closer to the pigeons pecking at the ground. A cautious third step brought her in amongst the outsiders. They seemed not to notice. Just one more and she would be deep in their midst. She gathered up her new dress, and stepped.

Without warning, two hundred pigeons took to the air in an updraft of wind and feathers. Terrified, Molly caught her breath. She turned her head to look at her parents, seeking reassurance. They were smiling, mockingly so. Her older brother, Charlie, was actually laughing.

There was a man in uniform. A big man with white hair. He had been with them all afternoon, telling them things about London.

"Did they frighten you, little Miss Molly?" he said.

She held her breath again.

"You see, when Lord Nelson shifts his weight from one foot to another, the pigeons feel it and take off. He's alive you know," said the man, nodding in the direction of the great column with the tiny figure on top. "And one day they will all come to life and take over the World."

The man coughed and spat out his laughter as he walked on. Molly looked up squinting against the sunlight. She knew the statue was staring down on her, and she felt she had been told a secret that she ought not to know. This was the worst birthday ever.

Some years later …

The Members' Lobby sits between Central Lobby and the House of Commons Chamber. It's a large square room, mainly in marble, and features the statues of former Prime Ministers. It's also an area where MPs collect their messages and important papers, and hang around chatting before going into Chamber.

Standing in bronze, with his hands on his hips, is Sir Winston Churchill. Prime Minister during the Second World War and perhaps looked upon as a one of Britain's heroes; what with all that he did for the country. Whereas the whole of him is a crinkly, dull, brown texture, his left shoe has been polished to a lighter colour. It's as if he's wearing odd shoes. It is said that touching his foot brings an MP good luck as they enter the Chamber, and over the decades this has made it shiny.

The MP for Oldham was about to do just that. He reached out with his left hand, one eye on where he was going and the other on Winston's shoe.

The shoe moved.

The MP looked up into the face of the statue, with his left hand suspended over where the shoe had been. His brain tried to comprehend what had just happened.

The statue of Winston Churchill has actually pulled his foot back.

Oldham's Member of Parliament wanted to fall over. He stood with his mouth open. Other MPs were also motionless, open mouthed, as if copying him. It was obvious that the shoe was now in a different position.

The statue moved again.

Slowly and stiffly, Churchill started to straighten up. Still with his hands on his hips, he turned his head cautiously, as if suffering from an old neck injury.

The MP uttered something incomprehensible. Surely, this must be some sort of stunt, the prime minister trying to get everyone's attention about something or other. There, he thought, the Prime Minister is just entering the room, right on cue; clever, very clever indeed.

What was even more clever was when the statue spoke.

"Since when has the MP for Oldham had to rely on luck?" said the statue.

The MP fell into a seated position on the floor as if simply knocked down by the voice. He looked at the Prime Minister seeking some confirmation that all this was his doing. The Prime Minister was looking just as stunned.

There was movement next to the PM. A bodyguard was pulling out his gun.

"Armed Police. Keep still."

The bodyguard held the gun out in front of him with both hands. He pointed it at the statue of Churchill then at the MP for Oldham, as if not quite sure of the real threat.

"Clear the room, clear the room," someone else shouted.

Another bodyguard appeared and immediately took up a position in front of the Prime Minister. The PM was ushered out through the doorway while being steered in a crouched position and looking as if something was about to drop on his head.

This was complete madness.

The MP for Oldham wondered if it was all his fault.

The statue of Winston Churchill appeared to be smiling.

Within the hour, the prime minister was staring intently at the statue. His personal bodyguards were present in the room along with several other armed officers. Winston Churchill had asked for a glass of cognac and a cigar, stating that he knew of the no-smoking policy, but as it had been a while, perhaps they could make an exception. Under the circumstances, no one felt in a position to argue. In fact, several of the MP's were only too willing to join him.

Everyone had shaken his hand, as much because it was Sir Winston Churchill as to see what it actually felt like.

The PM had hurriedly gathered a handful of key politicians and Sir Winston into one of the Select Committee rooms, keeping away from rooms ten and fourteen, which were wired with cameras and sound. He had given instruction that for the time being, the broadcast from the Chamber was to 'experience technical difficulties' knowing that this couldn't possibly go out live, not until they understood what the hell it was they were dealing with. He was confident the incident had been contained, but there was no way the public could handle something like this. It was unprecedented, and had to be kept secret.

There was chatter in the room from nervousness on the part of the MPs some of whom made silly jokes and comments about the situation.

Churchill was looking stern. He was answering their simple questions, and this was beginning to irritate him. It became clear when he'd had enough and wanted to say something. He paused to allow the cigar smoke to clear from in front of his face, and to ensure he had their undivided attention. The room fell silent.

"Who, could possibly have, ever, imagined?" he said. His delivery was easily recognisable. Slow but powerful as he punched out the individual words. Panning his hand around the room, still with the cigar between his fingers, he looked from person to person.

"I shall try and explain what is happening here, and then answer your questions," the statue said.

There was a noticeable sigh of relief around the room.

"When I died, I went to a place. It was not here. It was not England. It is difficult to describe. However, when you erected this statue of me, I became aware of what was here and what was going on around me. I could see and hear things, understand things. I have been doing so, ever since."

The voice was definitely that of Winston Churchill. When he moved, it was almost like a living person, just slower and with fewer actions. The bronze he was made from appeared to mould to his movements, solid but pliable. There were fewer facial expressions and when he spoke, there was little lip movement, as though he was imitating a poor ventriloquist. There was also no evidence, such as a rising and falling of his chest, that he was breathing.

The MPs sat in silence. One or two looked at each other, perhaps reassuring glances to check that this was real and they hadn't fallen asleep during Prime Minister's Question Time, and that this was some bizarre dream.

"We have been amongst you for centuries," said Churchill. "Not in a physical sense, call us spirits, or an energy source, but something happens to the human soul when it is embodied as a statue or sculpture. It is as though it creates a connection, a link between two worlds. A higher, more informative and advanced world, and here. That link also opens up a telepathic communication between all statues, and we are able to share thoughts and knowledge."

The statue rapped his knuckles on his metal chest. "You haven't discovered yet how to control the molecules of solid objects but that is exactly what I am doing right now."

The prime minister wanted to ask a question.

Churchill spoke again, "You're going to ask why I am here? There will be others like me. Other statues will come to life this morning, to help give you a message. An important message, and so important that it was necessary to get your attention in such a way that you would take the message seriously. Something so unbelievable that you would be left in no doubt."

Churchill paused for a moment as part of his build up.

"The World is coming to an end," he said. "The balance of the natural world, of all things living, has tipped."

There was another short pause.

"Over the years, we have listened to your plans on conservation. Your thoughts on the control of pollution, of greenhouse gases, combustion, the ozone layer, deforestation. What you are doing, it isn't enough. If your actions were just leading to some major catastrophe — we wouldn't get involved, it wouldn't be our place to. But this isn't just some disaster. It is leading to The End. As a species, you are going to be wiped out, and even though some may initially survive, they too will perish."

A silent alarm showed on everyone's face. This was incredible, unbelievably incredible.

The prime minister spoke. "How long have we got?"

"Not long," said Churchill.

"How about you stop looking out of that window and come and give me a hand," said her mother.

It was dark outside and Molly was staring through their bay-fronted window, a typical feature of north London houses, into the blackness. It was also raining, and she had been racing the beads of water down the glass.

"Come on Molly," said her mother as she placed a pile of paper napkins on the table. "The guests will be here soon."

Molly didn't want the guests to be here, soon or otherwise.

"I thought you were going to wear something nice?"

Molly tutted. She placed the tip of a finger on the glass as if she could stop one of the beads of water from winning.

Her mother walked over to the window. "Am I to guess you're feeling a little sad?" she said, slipping an arm around Molly's shoulders and giving her squeeze.

There was an almost undetectable nod of Molly's head.

"Because we're going?

Another nod.

"You could have come with us, we did say."

Molly dropped her head and pouted. "I know. It's just, I'm going to miss you and Dad, that's all."

Her mother smiled, and stroked Molly's hair. "We know, and we'll miss you. We didn't take the decision to let you and your brother stay lightly, you know. You're only fifteen, no matter how grown up you feel. Come on now, help me put some snacks out."

Molly followed her mother into the kitchen.

Piled high on the small Formica-topped table were packets of crisps, peanuts, bacon chips and cheesy whirls. Normally, she would have plumped for this job, tearing open packets and sampling the contents as she tipped them into bowls. Right now, she felt that her stomach had a 'closed' sign and was unable to function, even with the smell of hot sausage rolls coming from the oven.

She thought back to the family chats they'd had, when she had opted to stay behind with her brother; while Mum and Dad went off to South America as part of their work as conservationists. It would be the first time for Molly, not to go. She had felt so confident, boasting to her friends that she had chosen to stay in London. It didn't feel such a good idea now, as they prepared for a party for her parents' departure. Party is what they were calling it; there would be more discussion than dancing, and party politics rather than party games.

Before long, the doorbell was ringing with each guest's arrival. This led to: an opening of the front door, a stamping of cold feet, shaking of dripping umbrella, disposal of wet outer garments, and hugs and kisses with her parents. Guests brought bottles of wine and sometimes a small, decoratively wrapped gift. Molly watched from the sitting room, which gave a good view out onto the street as well as into the hallway and the front door. All the guests were well dressed, some of the men were wearing jackets, one or two with ties. Molly wondered if she should to go to her room to change but decided it would be difficult to come down again.

She shook hands with some, nodded at others, and repeatedly smiled when told she was so much more grown up than the last time they saw her. Mum and Dad had an odd assortment of friends, mainly from the university where they worked; academics, scientists and especially conservationists.

Molly fetched, carried, and topped up wine glasses, including one of her own.

"Where is that brother of yours?" said her mother.

Charlie was still out despite promising that he would be home at a reasonable hour.

"We suspect he's got a girlfriend," said Molly's dad to everyone in the room. "About time too, at seventeen."

Guests smiled and nodded.

Molly had suspected the same. She hadn't asked him directly; sometimes he might meet someone he fancied, rather than actually getting to go out with them, but recently he had been a bit distracted.

The doorbell rang.

Dad chuckled. "Right on cue," he said. "Another one who can't remember to take a key." He ruffled the top of Molly's hair as he walked past.

As he turned the catch, a gust of wind forced open the door, and was followed by a spray of rain. Everyone peered down the hallway to the front door as Dad stepped back, staring at the doorbell ringer.

"Good God," he said.

"What-ho, Hargreaves," said a strong and powerful voice. An outstretched hand appeared clutching a bottle of wine, and then a large man stepped in. Sliding a soaking wet raincoat from his shoulders, the new guest enthusiastically shook hands with Molly's father, and then reclaimed the bottle of wine by holding it to his chest. He walked into the sitting room.

"Where's that lovely Mrs Hargreaves, then?" he said.

Molly's mother looked just as stunned. "Oh my goodness, Gee-Gee?" She said the name is if asking the man to confirm his identity. Even so, they hugged and kissed each other on the cheek.

Some of the others guests knew him, and they stood to shake his hand, others were quizzical, but it was clear that Gee-Gee had not been seen for a long time.

Molly hadn't seen him before in her life, as far as she could remember, and she thought she would remember. He was a such big man, with big hands and big feet, broad shoulders, unkempt white hair and a solid looking head. Even his teeth looked bigger than they ought to.

Her dad reappeared, wiping his hands dry after hanging up the wet coat. He walked over to Gee-Gee, who was now standing with his back to the fireplace, as if warming himself, even though the fire was unlit.

"For those that don't know this gentleman," said Molly's dad to everyone in the room, "this is Gee-Gee, a long time friend, not seen in ages, historian, traveller and an authority on all things weird."

Everyone laughed.

Someone handed Gee-Gee a large glass of red wine, which he held up in toast to everyone in the room.

"So tell us," said Dad, "where the hell have you been, what have you doing?"

For the next hour, Gee-Gee did just that. No one else got much of a word in, even when he paused to gulp wine, which was often. Molly listened with curiosity. Several times, she caught herself staring at Gee-Gee, as much because of his unusual features as because of what he was saying.

"Take Edith Cavell," said Gee-Gee.

There was a discussion going on about being famous.

"Shot in 1915, after being caught in Brussels helping British and French soldiers to escape. Patriotism is not enough, she said, I must have no bitterness or hatred towards anyone. Now, there's no doubt that she was a brave woman, working as a nurse in difficult times, but the allies used her execution as propaganda, increasing recruitment in America. Was she a hero, or heroine, or whatever is politically correct these days, or a result of the media?"

"She also said," quoted one of the guests, "that she didn't want to be remembered as a martyr or heroine, but simply as a nurse who did her duty."

Molly had read about Nurse Cavell. She wondered if she would have the courage to cope in a crisis such as a war. Would she be frightened, would she be determined? Would she know what to do and when? She didn't believe she'd be the sort of girl who would just stand there and scream.

"Do you want to be famous?" said Gee-Gee.

Molly looked up and realised he was talking to her. It was the first time he had acknowledged she was there, and now everyone was looking at her. She felt a warmth start to rise around her neck and into her cheeks.

"I don't know," she said rather weakly.

"Well, what do you want to do when you grow up?"

Molly didn't know that either.

"She wants to work with animals," said her mother. "She's always been good with them. She's just got a weekend job at a pet shop."

Several of the guests were smiling and nodding, as if accepting that this was a perfectly good thing to want to do.

That was not the answer Molly wanted to give. "I want to do something worthwhile," she said.

The smiling and nodding stopped.

"Such as?" said Gee-Gee.

"To help somewhere, to discover something," she shrugged. "I don't know, to save someone."

"There you have it," said Gee-Gee to the whole room, "even at her age, she wants to be famous." He took a wine bottle from the mantelpiece and refilled his glass. He looked content that he had proven his case.

"That's not what I said." Molly clenched her fists into her lap.

Gee-Gee paused with glass in one hand and bottle in the other.

"I said I wanted to do something worthwhile. To do something with my life." Molly realised she might be in danger of implying that everyone else in the room hadn't done anything with their lives. "I'm really lucky to have done the things I have done already, with Mum and Dad and some of their friends." She gave a quick glance around the room. "I want to make good use of the things I have learned." She looked up at Gee-Gee. "That doesn't mean I have to be famous. I disagree with what you've said about Edith Cavell. She didn't have to become a nurse, she didn't have to go and work in Belgium during a war, and she didn't choose to save soldiers because she wanted to be famous. The fact the media make her famous, doesn't make her any less of a worthy person."

"But how much of what she did, is true?" said Gee-Gee, "or was it hyped up to alienate the Germans? You can't answer that, can you, little Miss Molly Hargreaves?"

The wine bottle still in his hand, Gee-Gee refilled his already full glass. The red wine overflowed, cascading onto the carpet, and catching some of the nearby guests on the way down.

Molly wasn't sorry he'd done it.

There was a sudden burst of activity in cleaning up, with several suggestions as to how to deal with spilt wine. Salt, was her mother's choice.

The carpet around Gee-Gee's feet quickly became a miniature salt mountain scene at sunset. It was obvious to all that Gee-Gee had drunk too much, and some of the guests made movements to leave. It was getting late — thank you so much for the party — have a great trip. Just as quickly as they had all arrived, they were all gone. All except Gee-Gee, who had taken no part in tidying up, but had emptied and refilled his glass instead.

"When do you leave then?" Gee-Gee asked her dad, who was just getting comfortable on the sofa with his right arm curled round the back of it.

"Monday. We've got the weekend to sort out the equipment we're taking and get packed."

Molly started to collect the used napkins and cocktail sticks.

"And what do you think about going back to South America, young Miss Hargreaves?" said Gee-Gee. "You know, it must be eight or nine years since I last saw you. You were a wee pup then," Gee-Gee continued without giving Molly time to answer his first question. "I don't suppose you remember me?"

Molly shook her head.

"The kids aren't going," said Dad. "We feel they're old enough to make their own decisions and they want to stay here."

Gee-Gee looked alarmed. "Good God, man, that's ridiculous. They must go."

Molly's parents looked puzzled.

"The family should stay together, is what I mean. London's not a safe place at the moment."

"What do you mean, at the moment?" said her father.

For the first time that evening, Gee-Gee looked flustered and lost for words. "Look, Hargreaves," he said putting down his glass. "I can't explain but I must urge you to take your two with you." His faced relaxed a little as if changing tack. "Trust me, take the kids and you'll all have a great time in South America. I insist."

"What are you not saying?" said Molly's mother, she turned to see Molly's reaction.

"Nothing, I just think it's important you all go," said Gee-Gee.

"Is it terrorism?" said Dad.

"No, no, it's ..."

"What is it then?"

"Look, Hargreaves, it's not that I'm a part of it anymore, but the Agalmata—"

"Oh no, for goodness sake, Gee-Gee, not that damn Agalmata thing again?" said Dad, getting up. "Come on you, you've had enough to drink, it was brilliant to see you, really, thank you for dropping in." He placed his arm around Gee-Gee's shoulders and steered him towards the front door.

Just as he was leaving, Gee-Gee turned to face Molly's dad. "You may have chosen to forget but ..."

Dad pushed him outside and followed, with Gee-Gee managing a hasty wave and quick goodbye as Dad pulled the door closed behind him.

Molly looked at her mother for an explanation.

"I wish your brother would hurry up home," said her mother, as she collected more empty wine glasses.

Molly could hear the two men discussing something outside. Then it went quiet, followed by Dad coming back in. His hair was glistening with the rain and he had rounded his shoulders against the chill.

"What's an Agalmata?" said Molly, still wanting an explanation of what had just occurred.

"Err, it's nothing to worry about," said Dad.

They had always encouraged Molly to ask questions and she knew he would have to provide some answer.

Her dad sighed. "Gee-Gee is someone we've known for a long time. He is a very clever man, a professor who used to work for the university and a holder of two doctorates. He's written any number of books. He got involved with some people, a sort of society who had some strange beliefs. In the end it cost him his job, his reputation, and nearly ruined…" He didn't finish the sentence.

Dad looked at Mum, with some concern.

"He's a friend of both of you?" said Molly, looking at each parent in turn.

"Well, yes, he was my professor when I was at university, so before you were born," said her father. "We've both worked with him at one time or another; he's had a hand in many pies. I wonder why he turned up tonight. You didn't invite him, did you dear?"

"Not at all," said Mum. "I haven't seen him in years, and I can't think who, out of our lot, would have invited him."

"Mmm, he usually has some reason for anything he does. Anyhow," said Dad, relaxing his quizzical look, "what a splendid evening."

The doorbell rang.

It was a wet, bedraggled and keyless, Charlie Hargreaves, who was sorry he had missed the party but was there anything left to eat.

It was one of those rare moments during the early hours of a morning in the Accident and Emergency Department of St Thomas' Hospital, when it all went quiet. Not empty, it was never empty, just quiet. Several of the cubicles were occupied with sleeping or resting patients; a nurse was re-stocking a cupboard with bandages and dressings; a doctor was catching up in writing his notes. Two porters were wheeling out a patient on a trol-ley. The patient had a drip in his arm, and was covered with a blanket, and one of the porters was telling him a joke.

A student nurse looked around for something to do. This was her first night shift with the A&E Department, and part of her on-going training, and she was keen to make a good impression.

A telephone on the desk rang. It was not a normal ring but one de-signed to be recognised and answered immediately. A staff nurse picked it up.

During the brief conversation, she took a few notes, said, "OK," sever-al times, and finished with, "We'll be ready." She replaced the receiver and then said in a loud voice, "Blue Call, adult male, five minutes."

The room came alive with people moving about.

The staff nurse explained to the student. "We've a motorcycle accident coming in. The switchboard will page the trauma team. That's made up of the A&E Consultant, an Anaesthetist, an Orthopaedic doctor and some of the nurses here. The casualty will be taken into the resuscitation room. You can come in and watch but don't get in the way."

As other medical staff were arriving, the student nurse spotted the ambulance pulling up outside, its flashing blue lights reflecting off the white painted walls.

Within one minute, the two sets of folding entrance doors automatically and noisily opened, and two Paramedics came in pushing a trolley. On the trolley was a young man wearing a smart, pinstriped suit that looked slept in. His cream coloured shirt had been pulled out from the top of his trousers and several top buttons had been undone. He had a supporting collar around his neck immobilising his head, and he had an oxygen mask over his mouth and nose. What you could see of his face was pallid, and his eyes were closed. He did not look well. The two Paramedics had an air of urgency about them as they concentrated on what they were doing.

This is Preston Morton," said the first Paramedic as he continued to push the trolley into a large room just to the left of the entrance. "Twenty-four years old, hit by a motorbike which bounced him into the roadside barrier. When we first got to him, he was conscious and complaining of pains around his kidneys, plus pain at the back of his neck. Motorcyclist is on his way in as well, mainly superficial."

Preston Morton was now in the resuscitation room and surrounded by the trauma team.

"On my three," said the other Paramedic. "One, two, three, slide."

Preston Morton was slid across on a sheet from the ambulance trolley and onto a bed. The trauma team set about him. Working in concert, they cut his clothes from his body, penetrated his skin with a needle and drew blood, attached pads and wires to his chest. A machine started to read his vital signs.

The student nurse was in awe. Seeing this on the telly was one thing;

real life was something very different. The harmony of the medical staff; the plight of the young man. She stood quietly at the back of the resuscitation room, and mouthed a short prayer.

"Pressure's dropping," said the anaesthetist. "Pulse two twenty." There was a frenzy of hands working on the patient.

"He's not breathing," said the anaesthetist. "We're losing his blood pressure."

"Right, one milligram of Epinephrine," said the Consultant. He spoke calmly and confidently, and was clearly in charge.

A nurse injected the drug into the cannula on the back of the patient's hand.

The student nurse was feeling uncomfortable. The room had become hot and stuffy, and she felt a little nauseous. She tried to focus on something else.

"Are you all right," said one of the nurses, looking up from what she was doing. "Why don't you go outside and get some air?"

The student nurse nodded. Relieved, she walked out of the resuscitation room, and headed for the ambulance entry doors. Pressing the large button on the wall, the doors opened and she crossed the small corridor, and stepped outside. Her eyes watered from the cold night air and there was a distinct dampness. She wrapped her blue cardigan tightly across her body. The yellow cross-hatchings and the painted words that said, Ambulance Only, had a ghostly colouring from the fluorescent-lit canopy.

There was a sudden and unfamiliar sound out in the darkness. It made her jump. Peering through watery eyes into the night, she searched for the cause. It occurred to her that perhaps Preston Morton had just died in the resuscitation room, and the noise might be his ghost coming to say a final good bye. She shivered at the thought, and decided to go back inside.

A figure appeared, to her right, just on the edge of the lighting. The student nurse was shocked to the spot. The figure was tall and strong looking. He had a droopy moustache. He was dressed as an old-fashioned soldier, wearing a pith helmet and with webbing across his chest. His boots had strapping running up each leg almost to the knee. Over his shoulder was a rifle.

The student nurse rubbed her eyes to get a better look.

The figure looked like a statue. Not because he was motionless and rigid, he wasn't, it was the bronze colour and texture of his skin and clothing that made him statue like. In his arms, being carried effortlessly, was another man. He had a similar colouring, and a similar moustache. He also had short hair, and wore an open necked shirt with the sleeves rolled up. He looked as though he was in pain.

"This man is injured," said the first soldier. "He needs a doctor."

The student nurse startled at his voice. She stared at the two soldiers, and then looked to her right and through the ambulance entrance doors. She could see the staff moving about inside the department. Perhaps there was a logical explanation as to why these two figures were dressed as statues. She took a step forward just as the first soldier started to lower the injured man to the ground.

"You can bring him inside," she said.

The soldier continued to place the injured man onto the ground, supporting the back of his head as he did so. The injured soldier was clutching his left side.

"Why are you dressed as statues?" she said.

"Help him," said the first soldier, "he has been in pain for a long time." His voice was gruff and she thought he might be a heavy smoker. Her left hand slipped into the front pocket of her uniform and found her new stethoscope. She fingered the tubing, considering whether to use it even if just to show she was prepared to do something.

In a simple and swift action, the soldier swung the rifle from his shoulder and jabbed it towards her. It had a bayonet on the end, as if a rifle wasn't menacing enough.

"Help him!" said the soldier.

Now, she was terrified. There was another sudden noise, this time behind her, and for a moment she thought she was about to be attacked. She turned to find Florence Nightingale. She had no doubt about this, all nursing staff knew what Florence Nightingale looked like; there was a statue of her just corridors away in the Central Hall, and St Thomas' was where she had started her nursing school. She even had the lamp in her right hand. She stared, transfixed, as Florence Nightingale walked up to the soldier holding the rifle, and gently touched his arm.

"Bring your friend, I shall care for him," said Nightingale.

The soldier gave her a sideways glance, hesitated, and then nimbly swung the rifle back onto his shoulder. He crouched down and scooped up his comrade, who was still clutching his side, turned, and disappeared into the darkness.

Florence Nightingale looked directly at the student nurse, scowling as if considering telling her off. She then followed the soldiers into the night.

The student nurse stood alone once more, still chilled from the night air. The ambulance entrance doors opened with their usual mechanical crash, and she let out a yelp.

It was a staff nurse from the resuscitation room.

"The patient's stabilised," she said. "You're going have to toughen up if you want to work in Casualty, you know.

Monday ...

Hampstead Heath is a pretty cool place to live, and at fifteen years of age, Molly was having a pretty cool life. For a start, she didn't go to school. So far, she had lived in Central and South America, visited the jungles of Borneo and Sumatra, and the only time she had gone to school was in Africa. There, the classrooms were made of wood, no glass in the windows and lessons started and finished with singing. Now living in London, her schooling was with her parents, the occasional tutor and her own studies. It's called home education, and Molly was aware that some people were sceptical of it working. She liked it. Sure, it took hard work and self-motivation, but she had grown up with that. Now it felt quite natural and even easy to pick up a book and study from it.

Sometimes, having read about something, she would go off and see it for herself, such as a place or a building. She could talk to people she met, ask questions and dig deeper than she could if she was just being taught in a classroom. This made it interesting and she understood things more easily. Her parents always tried to encourage such inquisitiveness. Charlie, her brother, also home educated, had done well in his exams. Of course, it helped having parents who were scientists, both of whom had achieved great things, with scientific discoveries to their names, including several new plant and insect species.

There was a down side. She had friends in different countries around the world, people she wrote to on email, or spoke to on one of the many internet chat sites, and it wasn't as though she had no one she could hang out with, but there was no real best friend. Her main friend was probably her brother. She wasn't sure that was home education, or because the family had moved around so much.

Not going to school meant she didn't suffer those Monday morning, school feelings or the last day of holidays. However, this Monday was different; Mum and Dad were leaving today, off on their scientific trip. An expedition to a remote part of the Amazon rainforest to measure carbon release from deforested soils. Not what governments were saying but what was actually happening.

Climbing out of bed, Molly threw on a pair of blue jeans and a long sleeved beige top; the same clothes she had worn the day before. She purposefully strode into the kitchen, put fresh coffee in the machine, eggs into boil, glasses of orange juice and cut bread poised in the toaster. Breakfast, ready for her parents.

It was just short of seven o'clock.

Charlie shuffled in, still wearing his pyjamas and sleepy eyes.

"Morning sis," he mumbled as he reached into the cupboard for a large breakfast bowl and the cereal box. Her brother was tall and lanky but ought not to be with the amount of food he ate. He looked at Molly's breakfast preparations.

"For Mum and Dad?" he said. "They've gone already,"

Molly felt despair.

"Not to the airport," he added. "There was a problem with some equipment and they've gone to the uni. They'll be back for their bags."

Molly stared at the boiling eggs.

Having tidied up after her breakfast and with her parents still away at the university, there was little for Molly to do but wait. She wandered back to her room, took a history book off the shelves, and allowed it to open on a page.

Queen Boudicca. On the death of her husband, King Prasutagus, Boudicca was publicly flogged and her two young daughters raped when the Romans failed to acknowledge that women could inherit.

The book had a drawing of Boudicca, the Queen of Iceni. There was a suggestion that she had been buried at Boudicca's Mound on Hampstead Heath. Molly had seen this mound while out walking and hadn't realised its significance. She made a mental note to go there again. Staring at the drawing of Boudicca, Molly tried to imagine the anger this woman must have felt. She was a queen but that hadn't stopped all the horrible things that happened to her and her daughters. The book went on to say that even the King's relatives had been enslaved. Molly pictured this strong, determined woman with waist-long, red hair, wading into battle. Probably covered in blood. Venting her anger on the Romans. Revenge must have felt good.

Molly's brother stuck his head round the door, "I'm making a drink, do you want anything?"

"Hey, do you know about Queen Boudicca?" said Molly coming out of her daydream.

"Yep, AD 60, led a revolt, beaten by the Romans, then got her own back by slaughtering everyone until they beat her again. Bit of a brute, wouldn't want to meet her on a dark night. Do you want something?"

"No thanks," said Molly.

Charlie hesitated in the doorway. "She used to pray to the Goddess Andraste, and release a hare just before battle. She made her battle plans according to which way the hare ran. Cool, eh?"

"Do you think I could be a Boudicca?"

Charlie looked surprised. "How do you mean?"

"Well, you know, strong and courageous, doing something outstanding?"

"What's brought this on?" said Charlie, stepping into the bedroom.

"I don't know. There was a man at Mum and Dad's party, asked me if I wanted to be famous."

"And do you?"

"No, well, yeah, maybe. Is that bad?"

"Depends. What way do you want to be famous?"

"I don't know. I want to do something special with my life. I think I'm meant to do something, I don't know, amazing."

"And you don't think you're doing that now? Ask yourself, how many other people do you know that have had the life you've had, apart from me?"

"What do you mean?"

You're born in Guatemala, you speak good Spanish, and you've travelled to all sorts of great places seeing all sorts of amazing things. You know what you've done. It's not your average life."

"But it feels average. I want something special to happen. I want to be known, no, not known, oh, I don't know. Anyway, it doesn't matter. Where were you all weekend, leaving me alone at the party with Mum and Dad's weirdoes? Anything you want to tell me, brother?"

"Nowhere special," he said. "Hey, Mum tells me you've got a job at a pet shop," he added, changing the subject.

"I haven't started yet, I just applied."

"What's that about?"

"I need the money. I also want to see how I feel about animals being sold in cages."

"And?"

"I've decided I'm only going to let nice people buy pets, and those who want them for the right reasons. Who is she then? Mum and Dad know you know?"

"What? Dunno what you're talking about?"

"Yeah, right." She pointed to her bed as somewhere for her brother to sit.

Charlie sat down. He was smirking. "Well, her name is Amber, and she's the older sister of Mark, you know, the guy who sometimes plays bass guitar at the centre. She came along one evening to listen to us play and we got on really well."

"How old is she?"

"Nineteen in December."

"Is she pretty?"

"Of course. Well, I think she is. I like her. We're playing again next weekend, come along and you can meet her."

"I might be more interested in coming along to meet Mark, her brother."

"Oh really," said Charlie, smirking again.

"Oh, oh, you just reminded me," said Molly. "Have you ever heard of the Agalmata, or something like that?"

"Agal what?" said Charlie. "No, I don't think so. Why?"

"There was a bit of funny scene at the party between Dad and the man that asked me about being famous. He said it. I can't quite remember what he said but Dad asked him to leave. Not in a horrible way. He was a bit drunk."

"Did you ask dad about it?"

"Yeah, course, he said it was nothing to worry about. The man was someone they'd worked with, but I've never heard of him before — Gee-Gee."

"That's his name, Gee-Gee?

"Yeah."

"Like the horse?"

"Suppose so."

"Did you check it out on the web?"

"What Gee-Gee?"

"No, Agalmata, you dummy."

"Good idea." Molly turned to her laptop on the desk.

"I'll grab a drink and be back in a minute," said Charlie and he left the bedroom.

Molly searched for Agalmata on the internet. She came up with some academic papers on Greeks, their Gods and their Statues.

In the kitchen, Charlie filled the kettle for a cup of tea. The radio was on, and he retuned it from his parents' taste of classical to something more listenable. A local London channel was broadcasting the news. He walked from the kitchen, across the hallway and stepped into the downstairs toilet to stare at his face in the mirror. He combed his hair with his fingers, picked at a small red spot on his chin, and wandered back just as the kettle was boiling.

"Police this morning are investigating a daring theft of one of the Capital's most famous statues," announced the radio. "The Royal Marines National Memorial in The Mall is missing." The reporter went on to describe the statue as one Marine stood over his injured comrade.

Charlie rummaged around in a cupboard looking for something to eat. "Inspector Smyth from the Metropolitan Police has said that there was likely to be a logical explanation, such as they had been taken away for cleaning. However, a spokesperson from the Council dismissed this, as statues were usually cleaned where there were," continued the report.

Charlie found some small Madeline style cakes.

The two morning-radio presenters made jokes about what might have happened to the statue and put forward ideas from acid rain to sophisticated gnome thieves. They discussed the clothing of that day, pith helmets and puttees, and they finished with a phone-in number for sightings of the missing statues.

Resupplied, Charlie climbed the stairs to Molly's bedroom.

"Anything on Agalmata?" he asked.

"Not much, something about Greeks and their Gods, I don't think that's what he was talking about," said Molly, not mentioning the statues.

It was mid morning by the time Molly's parents arrived home, in a whirlwind of excitement. Last minute packing, checking passports and tickets, and then tearing out the house with Molly and Charlie trying to keep up. They all took the tube to Heathrow and made their way to the terminal .

Molly liked airports, with their big, open areas, lots of people, cafés and shops and everyone doing something. She always felt they were places of emotion. People sad because someone was leaving or happy because someone was coming home. She could easily spend lots of time at airports, just watching everybody.

Today, she had mixed feelings. It was great that Mum and Dad had decided to leave them for this length of time; they were being trusted to be old enough to look out for themselves, but she was going to miss them. The good thing was that she would get to hang out with her brother, as he was in charge and responsible for looking after her.

While their parents were checking in with American Airlines flight to Lima, Peru, Molly and Charlie took a walk round the terminal. They ended up at Arrivals and stood staring at the travellers coming through. It was interesting to watch a crowd of people waiting behind the barrier, looking for their loved ones coming through. Molly put those waiting into three categories. First, there were those in suits, usually drivers and chauffeurs collecting businessmen and VIP's. They were the ones holding a sign saying Mr. so-and-so or such-and-such company. Most of them would have a mobile phone attachment clipped to one ear.

The next group were those who wanted to look nonchalant, as if they met someone at the airport most days of the week, usually wives meeting husbands, or grown-up sons meeting parents. They stood towards the back with their hands in their pockets as if bored or as if not really looking. Under the surface of course, they were as just as excited as the third group.

These were people not bothered about showing exactly how they felt. They would be pressed up against the barrier, heads bobbing in all directions, trying to get a glimpse behind the Arrivals' doors. When the people they were waiting for arrived, it would be arms out stretched, big grins and almost at the point of their feet leaving the ground.

For Molly, this was the best group. Sadly, she couldn't think of any trip she had come back from, where she or the family had been met by such welcomes. Whenever they had arrived at an airport, it had been someone from the university or a project manager that Mum and Dad had been working with who would greet them.

"Where do you reckon they've been?" said Charlie with a nod of his head towards a new invasion of people had just started to come through.

Molly studied them briefly. Mums with children, some in pushchairs, others running ahead out of control. Beer-bellied Dads, one or two wearing football shirts and lobster red faces. Lots of duty-free bags amongst them.

"Spain or one of the islands," she said.

Molly and Charlie had played this game many times before. That was an easy one.

Molly looked at the suits and the names they were holding up in front of them. She chose one.

"Ok," she said. "See who can pick out Mr Calvo before he makes himself known to that driver." She nodded towards a man in a dark blue jacket and tie and with the customary earpiece for his mobile phone. The sign he was holding said just that — Mr Calvo, except it was printed and not handwritten as many of the others were.

Charlie accepted the challenge and started to scan all the likely candidates. Molly analysed her brother's likely thought process. He could rule out the holidaymakers. Mr Calvo was an unusual name. It means bald in Spanish; would the man fit the name? The trick would be to spot someone looking for their name, their recognition when they saw it, and the reaction of the driver with the sign. Then to declare it first.

Molly spotted a possible. Tall, thin man, well dressed, with an air of importance. He was also bald. There, he had just moved his head to get a glimpse around someone immediately in front of him. She pointed him out to Charlie.

"What are you two up to?" said voice behind them.

Charlie and Molly turned round to find their mother. Dad was walking up behind her, stuffing passports and boarding cards into his hand luggage.

"Nothing," said Molly and Charlie simultaneously.

Molly and Charlie glanced back at the driver shaking hands with the tall, thin, bald man.

"One nil, I believe," said Molly as she chalked up an imaginary one in the air with a licked finger.

They followed their parents into a coffee shop.

Over drinks and a sandwich, Molly and Charlie listened to some final reminders about taking care of themselves; getting on with each other, and contacting the university if they needed to get in touch.

"Molly," said Mum, "I know you are very mature for your age, but Charlie is in charge. Look after each other, help each other. There's plenty of food in the freezer, and I've left some money for shopping."

Molly looked at her brother. His face showed no emotion as if trying to look serious about his responsibilities.

"Molly," said her mother, in a firmer tone.

Molly looked back at her mother.

"Spend some time with your friends. You don't have many and if you don't keep in contact you won't have any."

Molly looked up towards the ceiling. This was becoming a recent and familiar statement from her mother. Just because she didn't have close friends that telephoned or popped in all the time, her mother considered her daughter a loner. That wasn't the case. Molly felt comfortable talking and being with anyone. She was friends with everyone.

"I think you should both stay out of the City," said Dad all of a sudden.

"What?" said Mum as she tilted her head slightly to one side. "We live in the City."

"No, I just mean stay out of town, you know, they shouldn't go any-where that's dangerous."

The three of them studied Dad's face, trying to understand him.

Dad shrugged. "You know what I mean, take care."

There was no point in taking a long time to say their goodbyes and be-sides, their parents would be back again in a month. There were hugs all round, and Molly felt a tightness in her chest. As she walked away, she limited herself to just the one look and a wave, before she turned to catch up with her brother who was already several strides ahead.

"I wish we were going with them," she said.

"Being apart from your parents, Molly, is all part of growing up," he said.

Molly skipped alongside him. "Oh yeah, how would you know?"

"Don't worry, little sister, I'll look after you."

"Yeah, right," she said as she tried to trip him up but missed. "Espe-cially as you are intending to be famous."

Molly chased him towards the train station.

On the 16th June, 1919, the New York Times reported: *Alcock and Brown fly across the Atlantic; make 1980 miles in 16 hours, 12 minutes; sometimes upside down in dense, icy fog.*

Captain John Alcock and Lieutenant Arthur Whitten Brown became instant heroes. They were given a prize of £10,000 from Lord North-cliffe's Daily Mail, which was presented to them by Winston Churchill, Britain's Secretary of State. A few days later, both men were knighted at Buckingham Palace by King George V.

You could say they had a great sense for adventure.

There is a statue of Alcock and Brown outside the Heathrow Academy, which is on the Northern Perimeter Road at Heathrow Airport. The two men stand locked together in a white coloured stone. Both men are wearing flying jackets and caps with goggles. Alcock has one of his flying gloves in his hand and Brown is holding a book.

There are two runways at Heathrow airport, the northern and the southern but both run east west. One is used for landing, the other for take offs.

American Airlines flight to Lima, Peru, via JFK in New York, was now at the end of runway. Heathrow Tower had given permission for it to take off. The pilots had run through all the pre-flight checks, and now with a hand each on the throttle quadrant they eased it forward. The pair of Rolls Royce engines easily produced the power for the plane to reach 165 mph, and the point of no return, as at the speed the plane could no longer safely abort the take off.

Something caught the captain's eye.

While hurtling down the runway, concentrating on the task at hand, he spotted two white figures crossing from the perimeter fencing and onto the runway. The captain cursed aloud; braking or swerving was not an option. The two figures stopped on the runway as if watching the approaching plane. One had his hands on his hips, the other was holding a book. The captain and co-pilot pushed the engines harder.

At 180 mph, the air flowing over the wings was enough to make the plane airborne. The captain lifted the nose of the aircraft and it took to the air. Mercifully, there was no impact. The captain looked at his co-pilot, as if questioning that he had seen the same thing. He didn't wait for confirmation. He thumbed the radio switch.

"Heathrow Tower, American-one-three-one, over."

Heathrow Tower acknowledged their American Airlines call sign.

"Be advised, there are two ..." the captain hesitated, "two persons inside the perimeter, and crossing runway zero nine left, over?"

The air traffic controller receiving the call, immediately informed the Tower Supervisor, who swivelled his chair round to a pair of giro stabilised, mounted binoculars. His next action was to pick up the red phone sitting on his desk.

Simultaneously, alarms sounded in the control rooms of the Metropolitan Police, who have a station at Heathrow, and in the Star Centre, which is the control room for the British Airports Authority — the BAA. The alarm notified them of an Aircraft Ground Incident.

An AGI is about as serious as it can get.

Police call signs, Hunter Five-Zero-One and Hunter Five-Zero-Three, both armed response units, were in the police canteen having their lunch. A plastic cup of tea and a greasy fried egg came together on the plate, as the officers tore out of the building to get to their cars. Engines revving, they waited for the automatic gates of the police yard to open. The two police cars, both silver BMWs, turned out onto the main road and immediately switched on blue strobes, flashing headlights and sirens. Both drivers accelerated as the queue of vehicles ahead of them started to peel to either side to allow the police vehicles through.

The meeting place was Rendezvous Point North, a large, square area alongside the Northern Perimeter Road, and a stone's throw from the Heathrow Academy. Within minutes, the area was swamped with police officers and other staff. This intrusion could be anything from a refugee attempting to get into the UK, and they dealt with plenty of those, to a full-blown terrorist attack. They weren't taking any chances.

A police van pulled up and as the back doors were opened, a police dog bounded out ready for action, it looked hungry for a chase. An armoured vehicle, known as a Jankel, turned off the perimeter road, mounted the pavement and entered the secure area. Its six litres, V turbo diesel engine, producing three hundred and twenty-five brake horsepower, growled as it powered its way to the head of the convoy of men and vehicles about to search the area. This vehicle meant serious business.

The police Inspector started the search in the immediate area, and sent another team over to the aircraft hangers. He was waiting for a full description of the two intruders, having radioed for more information.

Heathrow Tower had informed all other aircraft to hold on the inner and outer taxiways, and as they stacked up, to wait at their stands. The departure boards began to flip over and show 'Delayed'.

The Tower Supervisor informed the Airport Duty Manager and his staff over the radio, and they confirmed their attendance. The London Fire Brigade, the London Ambulance Service and the Airport Fire Service were also called. There was no fire and no one was injured, but this was standard procedure.

The air traffic controller pressed his floor pedal opening up his microphone to speak.

"American-one-three-one, Heathrow Tower, over."

The pilot of the American Airlines Boeing answered his call-sign.

"American-one-three-one," repeated the air traffic controller, "are you in a position to supply a description of the two people, over?"

There was silence.

"American-one-three-one, please acknowledge."

The captain came on the air. "American-one-three-one, be advised, the two persons seen inside the perimeter, were the statues of Captain Alcock and Lieutenant Brown from outside the Academy, over."

"American-one-three-one," said the air traffic controller. "You mean were *dressed* as statues of Alcock and Brown, over?"

"That's a negative," said the captain. "There were the living statues of Alcock and Brown."

The air traffic controller stood up and threw his headset down on the desk in front of him. He looked at the Tower Supervisor. "What is this, some kind of bloody joke?"

The house seemed empty as Molly and Charlie arrived home. Charlie went straight to his bedroom, and despite using headphones, Molly could still hear the screeching of the metal strings of his electric guitar. Charlie was into his music, in fact, he was much artier than the rest of the family.

Molly stood in the hallway pretending her parents were still milling about the place. She listened for their familiar sounds. It seemed strange to think that before long, they would no longer be on the same continent. She wished she'd made more of her goodbyes.

There was a gentle knock on the front door. Not convinced that some-one was actually there, Molly cautiously opened it to find a skinny girl with dyed-reddish hair. She had a pale complexion and was dressed up: wearing a short skirt, three-quarter length black leggings, silky top and little heavy on the make-up. Her shoes were flat-soled and gold in colour and around her neck was a necklace of amber coloured stones, which could be clearly seen as her hair was up.

She must have the wrong address, thought Molly.

"Hello," said the girl. "You must be Molly." She extended her hand.

Confused, Molly shook it.

"I'm Amber. May I see Charlie, please?"

Molly would never have guessed. The girl certainly didn't look nearly nineteen. She stepped back to allow Amber in. "He's in his room," she said.

The girl didn't move.

"I'll take you up there if you like?" Molly led Amber upstairs to Charlie's bedroom, and noticed Amber glancing into every room they passed. So, she hasn't been here before.

Molly knocked quietly on her brother's bedroom door, and suspecting that he wouldn't hear, she turned the handle.

Inside Charlie was performing. Wearing a red bandana and stripped off to the waist, his skinny body showing a rack of ribs, he was oblivious of his surroundings except for his own imaginary audience.

Molly knocked again, now on the open door.

"Hey," said Charlie, lifting the guitar strap over his head as he grabbed a tee shirt and stepped forward to welcome his guest, all in the same movement. "How are you?" he said to Amber, easing her into the room and Molly out, and then closing the door.

Molly smiled and went to her own room. She sat for a moment and thought about how she felt about her brother having a steady girlfriend. Charlie was a good brother, kind and sharing, he had become a real friend. He was strong, practical and knew how to work hard. She had seen how he had helped out when their parents were on expedition. Setting up camp, fetching water and supplies.

Appearance wise, he was more like their father than their mother, adopting his dark hair colouring and thin facial features. Molly had their mother's blonde curls and rounder, softer face.

She wasn't sure about Amber. She didn't seem to be the sort of girl that her brother would have chosen, not in appearance anyway. She picked up her history book again and thumbed the pages.

Before very long, Molly heard someone going downstairs. She wondered if Amber was leaving already. Seconds later Charlie stuck his head around her door, he looked slightly uncomfortable.

"We're going into town, to get pizza or something. You can come if you want?" he said.

Molly thought about being in the house on her own and agreed to go.

Charlie lowered his voice. "What do you think of her?" he said. "She's nice, isn't she?"

"Err, yeah" said Molly whispering, "but I've only met her at the front door. She's very pale."

The train from Reading was just pulling into the Platform. Isambard

Kingdom Brunel decided it was time. He stood up, put on his hat and brushed an imaginary piece of soot from the lapel of his bronze coat. The doors of the Reading train opened and like oil being poured from a can as commuters and tourists flooded out. Brunel stood beneath the clock with his hands behind his back, awaiting the reaction.

There was none. Well, none to speak of. People looked and some stared but the majority hustled on by. Other trains to catch, getting to the office, too much work, and too little sleep. Those who actually noticed that Brunel was not in his usual place gave it little consideration. They thought little more when the statue moved. Some may have considered stopping to see what he was advertising, if they'd had the time.

The statue of Brunel showed the palms of his hands in a *what the heck* type gesture, but still the people walked on by. He was the man who had built railways, bridges and tunnels, not to mention ships such as the SS Great Britain, the world's first iron-hulled, screw-propeller-driven, steam-powered passenger liner. Nearly one hundred and fifty years since he was last here, and no one uttered a word. He sat back down on his chair, situated at one of the exits next to the ticket machines. He would need to let Churchill know.

Florence Nightingale was to have more luck. She came alive on her plinth at the lower end of Regent Street. She'd already been active, earlier that morning when her other version in St Thomas' Hospital, had to intervene when the marines pulled their stunt. A glitch, those marines coming to life, not part of the plan. A seized opportunity to help an injured comrade. Still, no harm done.

Despite the over-cladding of her bulky dress, she climbed down easily and stepped onto the street. She fully understood the impact she was going to have on people passing by. They would be seeing something that their minds just couldn't comprehend. It was quite strange for the statues as well, but then that whole life after death thing was strange.

By the time Florence Nightingale had reached the ground, several pedestrians had stopped, gawping, mouths open. There was a man now sitting on the pavement, his arms supporting him from behind, he'd obviously fallen over with the shock. She hoped he wasn't going to do something stupid, such as clutching his chest or passing out. She didn't want to start the day administering first aid.

Cars were braking. Several had stopped.

There was a dog, barking at her, annoying little yappy thing.

Florence clasped her hands in front of her and tried to smile, she wanted to look friendly and well-meaning. Well, as much as a piece of sculptured bronze could.

A man in a dark suit walked up to her and said, "Now that is amazing," as he rapped his knuckles on her left arm then stepped back in greater amazement.

"I'm a statue, what did you expect," she said to the man. She turned to face the growing crowd; she was ready to address them.

"I am Florence Nightingale," she said in a commanding voice.

A Japanese man with a large camera appeared in front of her. His Japanese wife shuffled herself forward to stand shoulder to shoulder with the statue. Nightingale gently pushed her to one side, and then faced the crowd again.

"I am Florence Nightingale," she said again. "I am a statue. I have come back from being dead. I know this is impossible for you to believe but it is true. I am here to help you."

Within no time at all, Florence had a large crowd around her and traffic in the surrounding streets was gridlocked. Police sirens could be heard approaching. At this rate, she would have to get back up onto her plinth to be heard.

Just around the corner, in his shaded spot on Leicester Square, William Shakespeare took a relaxed stance on getting people's attention. He sat down. Still high on his plinth, he sat swinging his legs over the edge and waving at people as they walked by. It made him laugh when some of them waved back. A man, staring while still walking forward, walked into someone else, they both fell over. A woman walking a dog then stumbled over them. She cried out and her dog nipped one of the men as he was try-ing to get to his feet. Shakespeare slapped his thigh in merriment. This was better than some of his own performances.

Before long, Leicester Square was shoulder to shoulder full of people. No one could move. It was time for the Bard to do something. He stood up and took a long, low bow to the crowd who whopped, cheered and clapped in appreciation. Some of the crowd had never read a piece of Shakespeare in their life; today they were his greatest fans. He started with a few of his favourite lines, that would show he was he back.

Molly, Charlie and Amber headed towards Hampstead tube station. Charlie had suggested that they go to Leicester Square as there were plen-ty of places to eat and they could decide if they wanted to go to the pictures or not.

Amber walked along, holding Charlie's hand, a gesture Molly was not accustomed to seeing. Molly had noted that her brother was now wearing a pair of brown leather shoes, his jeans looked pressed and was that a hint of gel in his hair? She tagged on behind the happy couple.

Walking passed a shop window, Molly caught a reflection of herself. She always knew she was a slightly bigger build than most girls of her age, but against Amber, she felt positively fat. She ran her fingers through her hair, straw coloured with a natural wave. She should have brushed it, but she never fussed about her hair. It was as it was. Dressing was the same. Without changing to go out, she had merely grabbed her denim jacket as she left the house. She had been ready to leave the minute her brother had invited her. They had been delayed by Amber who had wanted to put on more make-up.

Once on the train platform, Molly asked Amber about her family, and what she liked to do in her spare time. With each answer, Amber directed her comments at Charlie, as if Molly wasn't there. Perhaps that's what Amber really wanted.

Molly tried a different tact.

"Mum and Dad will be in the air by now," she said.

Charlie clarified, "Our parents are off to Peru, doing research."

Amber nodded, she knew. "How cool to have your parents go off like that and leave you on your own."

"They know we can look after ourselves," said Molly.

"Yes, but you're still only fifteen," said Amber. "I suppose you've got your brother to look out for you."

"I don't need—" started Molly.

"We've gotten used to all the travelling," said Charlie. "Living in different countries, moving about from one house to another. Our parents have always believed that having children shouldn't stop them doing what's important to them. It's good for us too, we get to see some pretty far out places and meet lots of cool people. They'd want us to do our own thing one day, when the time was right."

"Have you ever been to the jungle?" said Molly, guessing that Amber probably wouldn't be seen dead in such a place.

"No way," said Amber.

"It's just amazing, Charlie and I have been many times. On the last expedition we were on together," Molly was making it sound grander than it was, "we were in a remote jungle basin, in Borneo, cut off for weeks."

Amber looked at Charlie.

"It was pretty amazing," he said. "You should go if ever you get the chance."

Sensing an upper hand, Molly added, "I got this pendant in the jungle." She pulled out a yellow coloured stone on a leather cord around her neck. "It's made from the resin of a hardwood tree in South East Asia. A bit like your name, Amber."

Amber didn't understand.

"It's known as Dammar," said Charlie. "The locals use it to light fires, as it's flammable. We have to watch where Molly goes in case she busts into flames." He laughed, and so did Amber.

There was a clattering and rush of air as the tube train hurtled in, and the three of them stepped into a crowded carriage.

Someone, somewhere would have made that first telephone call to the Press, or to the police, maybe both. Then it went ballistic. Phones rang, text messages and photos were sent. Every reporter was on the case. Some were quicker than others. This was the biggest story, ever.

The coming of a prophet, weeping Madonna, aliens from outer space, and contact with ghosts — nothing, in the history of mankind was to be as profound as this. For a start, it wasn't an account of one or maybe two witnesses. There were thousands.

We interrupt this programme — breaking news — live from London — in a special report — the most unbelievable discovery ever. It's a hoax — no, it's real. No one could say for sure — living statues.

All forms of broadcast were showing the statue story. The skies over the city were filled with helicopters containing television crews. Pictures were being sent around the world, just as the world's Press were being sent to London.

There was live coverage of the three statues that had come to life; Brunel, Nightingale and Shakespeare. Brunel, now appreciating the atten-tion after his rocky start, was taking questions from the floor as well as giving details of life in his time. He was explaining, in some depth, how he designed the station they were all standing in.

In no time, the areas in and around Leicester Square and Piccadilly Circus had shut down, either by the police or just by the volume of people and vehicles. Sirens could be heard everywhere. The British Transport Police had closed Paddington station, leaving the existing crowd there as they were refusing to move. That meant displacing all the commuter trains trying to arrive. The outside streets were packed with people, all seeking a glimpse and a word with the statue.

People in the street were being interviewed as to what they had seen and their reaction. What did it mean? Why was this happening to us? Did the statues have a message?

Mobile phone use was at bursting point as everyone phoned to give or receive the details of what was happening. Photographs were snapped and pushed through the airways. Mobile phone companies were struggling to cope with the demand. If there was a service, it was anything but normal.

The first Molly, Charlie or Amber knew of any of this, was when the train driver announced that he was sorry for the inconvenience, but as there was a problem at Leicester Square, they would not be stopping, but going through to Charing Cross.

Then they stepped out above ground — into mayhem.

People, thousands of them. Charing Cross station's forecourt was full and overflowing. Out in the road, the Strand was a solid moving mass: a multi-coloured, writhing, head bobbing, collection of people who seemed to be moving slowly on a conveyor belt. Molly likened it to a memory of seeing hundreds of felled trees floating down a river. There was a surge of people behind them as another trainload was delivered to the surface. Molly tried to push back against them. It was a pointless exercise.

"Stick together," shouted Charlie as he reached out. He grabbed hold of Molly's jacket and pulled her towards him while still clutching Amber's hand.

They joined the floating forest.

A couple of times, Molly felt her feet leave the ground while still being carried along. She had never experienced anything like this. It was an incredible spectacle. Mobile phones and cameras were being held above heads, recording the event. People chatted and joked with each other. Some complained they were being crushed.

"What the hell is going on?" shouted Molly.

"It must be a bomb threat," said Charlie who was pressed in tight between two strangers.

"Statues," said one of the strangers, "living statues."

"What?" said Charlie, "what does that mean?"

Amber cried out. "My shoe! Charlie I've lost my shoe." She tried to turn and bend down to recover the missing gold coloured shoe.

"Leave it," shouted Charlie. "Whatever you do, don't fall over." He pulled on her hand to lift her upright.

He let go of Molly.

The shoe lost, Amber, now limping, started to cry. Charlie slipped his arm around her waist to support her and then searched the faces looking for his sister. He couldn't see her. He called out her name.

Someone in the crowd jokingly called out, imitating Charlie's voice, "Oh Molly, Molly, wherefore art thou Molly?"

Some of the side streets were being closed by police, the crowd being directed along a certain course. Then it splintered into three, some taking Waterloo Bridge, others Aldwych, and the rest remaining in Strand.

Charlie and Amber found themselves in Holborn, before the crowd had thinned enough for them to step out into a doorway. Amber's make-up had run, and she was now inconsolable. Charlie led her into a shop to give her some privacy. She blew her nose with his handkerchief and wiped her eyes, then pulled out her mobile. There were seven text and five missed calls. She listened to the messages.

"I've got to go home," she said, with the phone still to her ear. "It's my Mum calling, she says I've got to go home straight away."

Charlie turned and looked out of the shop window. The perfect solution right now would be to see Molly wandering passed, but it was never going to happen.

"Charlie!" Amber stamped her shoeless foot. "I want to go home, now!"

Molly pushed and jostled her way to one side and finally pulled herself free. She looked for Charlie but she was too short to see above more than a few rows. What to do now? She could hear her father's voice — when lost, go back to the last place you were together. That would be Charing Cross station, which was going to be impossible. If you cannot do that, go to the last place before that. That would be home. Molly didn't feel she could go home; she needed to know what was going on.

She stopped and spoke to a few people. What they were telling her just didn't make sense. One person showed her a news clip on his phone. What she saw was a living statue performer dressed as William Shakespeare on the back of a flat bed lorry. She didn't get it. She tried to ring Charlie on his mobile but got nothing but his voicemail.

She made her way towards the river and Victoria Embankment, still having to negotiate her way through crowds of people and vehicles. There were police everywhere and she could hear helicopters, occasionally snatching the sight of one as it passed between buildings. Emergency Services were trying to get through the gridlocked traffic; people looked excited, and some worried and concerned; there was an atmosphere of surrealism. Molly needed to think and make a plan. She stepped out of the confusion and into a park.

A cracked wooden sign told her she was entering the Victoria Embankment Gardens, Temple Section. It wasn't a big park. There was a central concrete pathway lined either side by lawns and flowerbeds. The beds were flowerless and the strategically placed waste bins were overflowing with fast food packaging. Tall trees made the park seem overcast, and a cool breeze was causing leaves to fall from their branches. As Molly walked along the pathway, she passed small gatherings of people standing, or seated on benches, but all huddled over mobile phones. Everyone seemed to be talking about statues. It was a little unnerving.

To her left was a large bronze statue of a man with a beard. In its left hand was a book and the right hand was behind its back. There was a group stood in front of it, and one or two walking around the base. Molly needed some answers. She stepped into the group and squeezed her way to the base of the statue.

William Edward Forster, she read on the plinth, *to his wisdom and courage England owes the Establishment throughout the land of a national system of elementary education.*

Molly didn't care much for statues. She found it odd that people built them, even back in Greek and Roman times. She didn't understand why a carved piece of stone should be worshiped or idolised, even if beautiful; and most of them weren't. In London, they were nearly all politicians and royalty, and Molly had often asked herself, what of other people who had achieved great things?

She chose a middle-aged woman in a business suit who was staring up at the statue to ask what the hell was going on.

"Excuse me," said Molly.

The woman gasped and put a hand to her open mouth. Other people cried out in alarm.

"He's moving!" someone shouted.

Molly turned.

The statue was moving.

William Edward Forster was now looking directly down at Molly. She backed into the crowd, pushing against the resistance of those moving forward. The statue moved again. In a slow action, the dark coloured metal moulding to its movements, it brought the book up and clutched it to its chest in a scholarly stance.

This was unbelievable. Molly felt light-headed and her stomach tightened as she tried to comprehend what was happening. Reality, everything she had learned in her life, seemed to be slipping away. This just cannot be true, but there it was, right before her eyes. The statue was moving.

Molly tried to push her way through the crowd but it was impossible. She felt a strange sensation as though her hearing and eyesight were beginning to fail.

The statue's head moved again, following her movements. It was watching her. She tried harder to escape but her legs felt weak, she was losing her control over them. Someone caught hold of her from behind and lifted her upright, keeping her within the circle of spectators as if she was their defence. She must have stumbled into a horror film, her actions now in slow motion to add to the suspense. The statue, playing its part, lifted its right hand out in front and pointed an outstretched finger at Molly. The crowd stared, all eyes were on this young girl.

The voice was loud, almost deafening, and very accusing.

"There's a girl, who chooses not to go to school. After all I have done for education."

The stifling air around her, held the sentiment of the crowd — shame on you, it said.

Molly broke. Arms flaying, she drove a path through them and into the open air.

Charlie was not happy. They had barely spoken during the journey to Swiss Cottage and Amber's house, and he had really struggled between getting Amber home, and finding his sister. Amber's embarrassing tantrum in the shop, hadn't made it any easier. He repeatedly tried to get hold of Molly, phoning on both his and Amber's phones. Both displayed, no service. Amber said he could phone from her house.

There were other escapees on the train. Charlie talked with someone claiming to have seen Florence Nightingale. It had been from a distance but her plinth in Lower Regent Street was empty at the time. Others were discussing what they had heard or seen on the news.

Amber's parents met them on the driveway to their house. Her mother was in tears having seen the live coverage on television.

"What on earth were you thinking?" she demanded, directing her question at Charlie. "Why would you put my little girl in danger?"

Charlie tried to explain that he hadn't known what was going on.

Her father was a little more understanding. He listened to what had happened, asked a few questions about what they had seen and heard, and then insisted that Charlie try to contact Molly. They all went indoors.

The television was already on. It was showing the events from a helicopter. Three statues, Brunel, Nightingale and Shakespeare were living, talking and walking, just the same as everyone else around them. If this is a hoax, it was the greatest ever on Earth. Charlie asked to use the telephone.

All over, Londoners were gathering. In the parks, around monuments, police stations and hospitals. Are we under attack? Is it some mass illusion? Are the statues possessed?

Business offices were emptying of staff as they drifted onto the streets, confused, amazed, looking for answers; no one quite sure what to make of it all. Some stayed indoors, entranced by their television sets and the internet, bewildered by what they saw. Business in the City was in danger of collapsing.

People gathered at other statues; statues that were still lifeless. People asked questions, prodded and poked; some took the opportunity to get drunk, and some climbed onto famous figures, trying to prompt a reaction. The police were inundated with calls.

The authorities tried to control the masses by closing roads, tube stations and bus routes. The military were put on stand-by. All emergency services were calling in any off-duty staff.

The television programmes were showing scenes on the street, interspersed with speculation. They showed the history of the individuals, their lives then, our world now, and the differences.

There wasn't anything, at this stage, about saving the planet.

The Prime Minister cut through it all as he appeared on television everywhere.

"Today, may be as enlightening, as when man discovered that the World is not flat," he said. His opening address was never going to be easy.

"What I can tell you is that a number of statues in London ..." he hesitated, his eyes dropped a fraction and he seemed a little unsure, "have come to life. Now, as incredible as that seems to all of us, this is not a hoax. I can also say, and let me make this absolutely clear, we are not in any danger from the statues.

"We have some senior, science and technology experts looking into the events of this morning. I, and other ministers, have been talking with the statue of a former Prime Minister. His message to us is clear and unambiguous. It is one of conservation and the need to act, to save our planet."

The Prime Minister's tone softened a little. "We do not have much time, and so I would ask you all to accept what is happening, as incredible as that is, and to work with us. I have detailed the efforts that the Party and I have been taking, and we shall be reviewing those with the help of the statues. They are here to help us. Let me just repeat that. They are here to help us.

"As far as we can ascertain, this awe-inspiring development today, has occurred only here in London. I shall be in touch with Heads of State from around the world, this is something that concerns every nation.

Clearly, this may have far reaching effects for all of us and may answer some of our oldest questions, as well as posing even more fundamental ones about life."

The Prime Minister went on with his reassurances that the public were not to be afraid. He also asked that everyone receive the guests with kindness and true British hospitality.

There was an onslaught of questions from journalists. The PM took one. "Prime Minister, we understand you have been speaking to Sir Winston Churchill. Has he, or anyone else, explained how this has happened?"

"I won't go into detail at this stage," said the Prime Minister. "Clearly, we shall want to look at this more closely, but it appears that their energy, or spiritual being has used the embodiment we have provided when we created them as statues, to come to life. Simply, amazing."

There was a second onslaught of questions.

"Will they be turning us to stone?"

"Will Churchill become a Member of your Cabinet?"

"Have they confirmed that there is a God?"

"Will you be talking to the statue of Baroness Thatcher?"

The PM turned and was gone, and the television programmes switched back to theorising and discussing. There were reports on which statues were alive, and the implications of others coming to life. There were camera crews at the three locations of living statues. All scheduled television programmes were cancelled.

Charlie had sat, stunned for the duration of the programme; probably, along with the rest of the world. Amber was still hugging her mother, curled up together on the sofa, both had been crying. Her father paced the lounge carpet.

"As head of this family I think I should do something," he said. "I'm not sure what, at the moment but I shall come up with something."

"You can take any such notions of doing something right out of you head," said Amber's mother. "This has nothing to do with us. It's for the authorities to deal with."

"I'm just pleased we don't live in the centre of town," said Amber's father as if searching for confirmation that they will be safe where they live.

"What were you kids doing in town anyway?" said Amber's mother, "aren't your parents away?"

Charlie nodded. He remembered Dad's instruction of not going into the City. So far he had managed to ignore his father's advice, lose his sister, and upset his girlfriend and her parents. He asked to use the phone again.

The Prime Minister had ordered the opening of COBR, the Cabinet Office Briefing Room, a secure and dedicated suite of rooms situated within Whitehall. Equipped with telephones, computers and video conference facilities, plus anything else you think you might need during a crisis. The staff were watching the media coverage, the closed circuit televisions around London and were in contact with all the Emergency Services and the military.

A small group of people had been set aside from the main task force, analysing events and predicting outcomes. In the past, COBR has been used during floods, acts of terrorism, epidemics and the occasional war; this crisis was something completely different.

The Prime Minister had approved the police proposal to move the three living statues to Hyde Park; it would allow them to control the situation without the disruption to traffic. They were still in the process of organising a couple of flat bed lorries and police escorts. The television stations were reporting on the logistics and the probable route, with suggested places to be, if you wanted to see them. Hyde Park started to fill and the surrounding roads were already rammed with people.

The Police Commissioner had requested to come to Parliament to meet Sir Winston Churchill, in the flesh, so to speak. The Prime Minister had wanted him to stay where he was needed, in charge of policing, but had finally agreed. The Commissioner had assured him that in his absence, his most senior officers were hurriedly putting together plans on how to manage London. Unsurprisingly, there were no Standard Operating Procedures or contingency plans for statues coming to life. Urgent meetings were being held. Traffic congestion and crowd control appeared to be the greatest problems so far, but there were also meetings with the tactical and terrorist branches. All possibilities were being covered.

All those charged with being in authority in London, knew that they had to move quickly. The statues had the potential of causing mass hysteria on their own, even without their 'End of the World' message.

Churchill rose from his chair. Spreading his hands, he rested his fingertips on the beech wood table. For the last couple of hours they had been talking conservation and the way forward. The phrase *tipping point,* had been used a lot adding a sense of urgency, but dealing with the day's events was having more impact than any message.

"I would like to introduce some other great minds into our debate," said Churchill. "People, who in their time did great things, and can offer you experience and wise counsel.

One of the ministers raised a hand.

"We thought that some of the other former Prime Ministers from the Member's Lobby would make an appearance. Disraeli, Balfour, Asquith, Bayes, Atlee or even Mrs Thatcher?"

"History will have told us that not all people see eye to eye. I have selected three who have the ability to work together and to serve you well," said Churchill. "Let us start with Sir Hugh Myddelton. Born in 1560, he was an alderman, banker, cloth maker and goldsmith, and became the Royal Jeweller under King James I. He was perhaps best known for his work on the New River, bringing fresh water into London, incidentally, much of it though pipes made from elm trees."

The ministers settled into their seats, this was going to be interesting.

"An incredible feat of engineering, gentlemen and one which met with a great deal of opposition from surrounding landowners at the time. Myddelton overcame all of that and at considerable financial cost to himself." Churchill allowed the appreciation of this man's work to be acknowledged before moving on.

"The next person I have chosen is Edward Jenner. Born in 1749, the son of a country vicar, he noticed that milkmaids suffered less with smallpox than others did. He developed a vaccination, vacca the Latin word for cow, and something he declined to patent so that it could be free to all.

Publicly ridiculed by the medical profession and the church. Smallpox was a horribly disfiguring and often fatal disease. I have no doubt that it was this man's altruistic contribution that allowed the World Health Organisation to declare the disease eradicated from the world in 1980."

There was an expectation in the air that some ministers might clap, accompanied by enthusiastic nodding in agreement of Churchill's chosen man.

"Finally, I would like to bring in Michael Faraday. Born in 1791, he received only a basic education, but created the laws of electrolysis, an early Bunsen burner and the chemical Benzene. He went on to improve the safety and performance of lighthouses, and, of course, the Faraday Effect with light. His work with electro-magnetism became the principles behind the transformer and the generator.

"Gentlemen, these three will help us in creating plans for the future, and I would appreciate if you would facilitate getting them here as soon as possible. Myddelton is on Islington Green, Jenner, now in Kensington Garden and Faraday is outside the Institute of Electrical Engineers, on the corner of Savoy Street."

There was a sense of relaxed calm around the room. Someone was in charge, someone was making decisions, and, so far, they were good ones.

Churchill put his hands behind his back and looked satisfied.

"How about whiskies all round?" he said.

Molly had tried stopping other people in the street to ask if their phones were working. Not many were and no one was prepared to let her make a call. She queued for ages to use a telephone box, only to reach the answer phone at home. She guessed that Charlie would be walking the streets looking for her or had headed for Amber's house.

Finally, Charlie made contact with a text message giving Amber's home number. Molly queued again at a phone box. They spoke excitedly, almost shouting at each other, relieved that they were both safe. Charlie filled in the details of everything he had seen on the television. Molly told the incredible story of having actually seen a living statue, although she missed out what it had said and how frightened she had been. She needed to talk that through with Charlie. Why had the statue picked her out and how did it know that she didn't go to school?

Amber's father could be heard in the background, insisting that Molly should make her way to their address. This was not what Molly wanted.

"Charlie, don't say anything in front of Amber's parents, but can you get away and back into town?"

"Sure," said Charlie.

"We'll never find each other in the crowds, do you remember when Dad took us to that demonstration?"

"I do."

"Meet you there."

It took Molly a lot longer than she thought it would, to get across to the American Embassy. On the way, she wondered if she should have been more specific as to where they were going to meet; Grosvenor Square is a big place. Molly reassured herself that they would find each other.

That was before she saw what looked like a thousand people in front of the embassy. She joined the back of the queue.

"Honey, are you here by yourself?" said an American woman, who was with her husband and five small children. "Where are your folks?" The woman held out an arm encouraging Molly to come towards her. "We just don't know what's going on, it looks like there's gonna be a whole heap a trouble. Where are you from, honey?"

"What is going on here?" said Molly.

The woman looked a little surprised. "Are you British?"

Molly nodded.

"Why, I guessed you'd be an American, along with the rest of us. Are you with them pro-test-ors?" said the woman with a flick of her head.

Molly had no idea what the woman was talking about and she looked about the crowd for a clue.

"We're here for our safety," said the woman. "We're trying to get to our embassy. This place has gone crazy, what with your statues an' all. We wanna be back on American soil."

The woman's husband and kids all nodded in unison.

"Most the people here are American. Then you British show up and start blaming us for the statues coming to life, saying it's our fault about conservation."

Molly spotted a group near to the embassy. They were wearing white overalls, work goggles and chemical masks and many had banners and placards.

"I'm sorry this is happening to you," said Molly. "I'm just here to meet my brother, I didn't know—"

"I don't mean to blame you, an' all," interrupted the woman. I know it's not your fault. You can stay here with us if you like."

The woman started to introduce her family.

Molly needed to get away. "I think I can see my brother," she said. "Yes, that's him over there. It was nice to meet all of you." Molly guided herself through the crowd moving away from the embassy making it easier for Charlie to find her. The other two obvious places would be to stand next to one of the two statues in Grosvenor Square: Franklin D. Roosevelt and Dwight D. Eisenhower. Molly didn't want to be near either.

She could see the statue of Roosevelt, standing on his plinth, overlooking the Square. He wasn't moving. Eisenhower's plinth is positioned at the front to the right of the embassy.

The plinth was empty.

Molly stuck to the left hand side of the Square, avoiding both the empty plinth and the protestors. The front of the building was being protected by American soldiers, lots of them. Barriers had been put up and there were men in suits and dark glasses, suspiciously wandering about behind the cordon.

Come on Charlie, where are you.

There was a sudden movement in the crowd, scuffling feet, bodies turning, someone cried out in alarm, someone else in authority. Three or four fleeing protestors scrambled away from the main group. Molly spotted a muzzled, Alsatian dog, and men in military uniforms, pushing through the crowd and grabbing hold of protestors. In his efforts to get away, one man ran headlong into Molly, sending her backwards to the pavement. The fall left her winded; the man got to his feet and without apology, ran off. The dog was barking, despite the muzzle; Molly was in danger of being trodden on, she needed to get to her feet.

"She's one," boomed a voice; male, American accent, someone in charge.

Molly looked up at the statue of Eisenhower who was standing over her, with his hands on his hips.

Two soldiers grabbed her arms tightly and lifted her to her feet. The dog, still barking was being held back on a tight leash. There was another soldier with a rifle or machine gun, Molly wasn't interested in the difference — he was pointing it at her.

"She's one," repeated the statue of Eisenhower. "I remember her," said the statue while pointing a bronze finger directly at Molly's chest. "She was here last month at the Eco protest, she's one of the organisers."

Terrified, Molly tried to pull her arms free. The soldiers held on tighter, their fingers digging into her skin. She tried to drop to the floor, but they supported her.

"What are you talking about?" she screamed at the statue. "Leave me alone, get your hands off me. Are you mad? I'm not with these people."

Her actions confirmed her guilt; the soldiers made their arrest.

"Lower that weapon," shouted a British voice.

Molly looked to her right. A Metropolitan police officer holding a handgun was standing to one side with two other colleagues. The crowd had given them room by backing off, it was obvious that this was getting out of hand.

"Lower that weapon," said the officer again. "You have no authority to deploy on the streets with a loaded weapon."

The American soldier did as he was told, acknowledging that he had over-stepped the mark. More police officers were arriving in transit vans, they jumped out and started to organise and control the crowd. Molly continued to protest her innocence and sensed she was getting through to them as the two soldiers had already let go of her arms. The statue had gone.

Then Charlie was there, in amongst them all, talking, explaining and promising to take her home. The police officers agreed, and Charlie ushered Molly through the crowds to a quiet street.

"Bloody hell, Molly. What was that all about?" he said. "I got here and they were pointing guns at you," he continued not giving her the chance to speak.

Molly was shaking.

"The statue knew we had been at the protests, you know, with Dad. How did it know that?" she pleaded.

"What statue, what are you on about?" said Charlie.

"Eisenhower, of course," said Molly.

"He was on his stand when I got there. Did he come alive then?"

"Yes, he was stood right over me and told the soldiers to arrest me." She explained exactly what had happened and what the statue of Forster had said in Temple Gardens.

"How do they know these things about me?"

Charlie shrugged. "I think maybe you're putting two and two together."

"Charlie!" Molly shoved her brother. "It doesn't make sense!"

"I haven't any answers, Molly," said Charlie calmly. "I don't know what's going on."

Molly slumped her aggressive stance. "I wished we'd chosen somewhere else to meet up."

Charlie smiled. "You still up for going to Hyde Park?"

"Too right."

They found the statue of Florence Nightingale at Speaker's Corner, in Hyde Park facing a huge crowd of people. Being taller than anyone else, the statue could be clearly seen, and was taking questions from the crowd.

The Press had quickly colonised the outer area to give it their best coverage, and cameras were broadcasting live pictures. There were a number of boom microphones on extendable, mechanical arms, which floated over the top of the audience and stopped when someone had a question to ask. A camera followed the boom mic and the image was displayed on large screens, as well as going out live around the world. The questions and answers were also being broadcasted over huge television screens. Occasionally, the sound or picture would be lost, but the organisers had done well to get the whole thing assembled in such a short time.

The evening was pleasantly warm for September with the setting sun reflecting off the clouds, all of which was adding to the spectacle. Molly and Charlie joined the edge of the crowd, and were quickly absorbed as more and more people arrived.

"Does it feel strange to come back?" was a question from someone towards the front.

"Absolutely," said the statue. "It's difficult to explain. I am sure you have all wondered, at one time or another, what happens to us when we die. When I passed away, I remember feeling a great calm. It was only afterwards that I realised that I was still thinking about things. It then became clear that I could communicate with others."

"Do you know that you are considered the pioneer of modern nursing?"

The statue lowered her head a little. "I am aware, and I am deeply honoured. Remember that during my time I had to deal with all types of prejudices in the nursing profession. I always believed in what I was doing, but it wasn't always easy to prove. If you take my work with the British Army, I had to confront not only British Generals but men of all ranks and standing, and in an age when women were meant to be devoted, obedient housewives and mothers."

The statue continued, "The attitude towards nurses as well, at that time, was such that they were considered as hanger-ons to the Army, on a level with the cooks, and believe me, much of the time I felt the road was up hill and very steep."

There was a round of applause from the crowd. One of the boom mics swung again and came to stop above a tall, young man.

"I understand that you managed to convince the authorities that the problems with the death rate in the Crimea could be objectively measured and subjected to mathematical analysis?"

"Are you a mathematician, sir?" said the statue.

"Yes, sort of," said the man, "I'm studying statistical analysis." There was a close up shot on the big screen of the man looking proud of himself.

"Then you'll know of my work with statistics and my polar area diagrams, which enabled me to plot the incidents of avoidable deaths that were occurring. I was able to reduce the death rate by introducing proper hygiene and cleanliness, and by keeping accurate records, then I demonstrated that what we were doing was the reason for the reduced number of deaths."

The cameras panned out to capture another hundred hands shooting into the air, all begging to ask the next question.

"What was it like in the Crimean war? Were you scared?"

"I think horrified would be a more apt description. Poor food, no sanitation, men with horrific injuries; not just physical injuries, but mental problems as well."

The boom mic swung again and came to rest directly over Molly, even though she didn't have her hand up. She stared up at it just as people were staring at her. She found something to ask. "Would you be so kind," said Molly in a polite voice, "to tell us about Mary Seacole?"

There was a hushed silence over the crowd. Someone nearby said, "Mary who?" The statue hesitated.

"She was a fine and well-meaning nurse," said the statue and looked to the crowd for the next question.

The boom mic stayed where it was, still over Molly's head.

"I believe she asked to come out to the Crimea with you but was repeatedly turned down, in the end she made it there on her own finances, and set up a hospital directly on the front line, looking after many of the wounded straight from the battlefield," said Molly in one long sentence. "She was originally from Jamaica."

"I did meet Mary Seacole, but that was out there," said the statue. "At the time she was applying to work in the Crimea, I had already departed. We all had our part to play. I don't expect, young lady, that in your life so far, you have had to experience such difficult times, and I hope you don't."

"In books on her," persisted Molly, "Mary states she thought it was to do with the colour of her skin."

There was a groan around the audience.

Charlie tugged the sleeve of Molly's jacket. "Where are you going with this, Molly?"

"Give it up," someone shouted from the crowd.

"Get a life," someone else called out.

It was not going well. Rather than leave it alone, Molly made it worse. With the thumb and index finger of both hands, she formed a 'W' above her head and loudly said, "Whatever."

It came up on the big screen, crystal clear.

The boom mic shifted and looked for the next question. The crowd around Molly closed again. She hadn't been very smart. By some miracle of science perhaps, the re-incarnation of Florence Nightingale, a heroine of her time and ours, appears as a living statue, and Molly tackles her on being racially prejudiced. No, she hadn't been very smart at all.

"You know this is all wrong," said Molly, throwing her denim jacket down and collapsing over the arm of the settee. She and her brother had been silent all the way home but she was ready to say something now. "Look at it this way, Mum and Dad have been involved in conservation all their lives, we know, we've been dragged half way round the world behind them. They set off this morning for another expedition, continuing their work. There was no sense of urgency— no good-byes forever— oh didn't we say the planet is on its last legs? Well, not as far as I could tell."

"We've always known there was something wrong," said Charlie. "At

some stage that has to go from being wrong but there's time to fix it, to —
there's something wrong and you're out of time."

"What if the statues are lying?"

"Lying? Why should they be lying?"

"Because they're here for something else."

"Like what? Look Molly, it's all pretty amazing. We've just discovered
that there is life after death. I mean, that's a question that has been asked
since time began. That in itself is mind-blowing let alone the fact that we
really are screwing up the planet. It's all going to take some getting used
to."

"What about Miss, I'm-not-so-cool, Nightingale?"

"Well, you did give her some pretty irritating questions and it was in
front of several billion viewers on live television. Most people would
have reacted in the same way. They're not aliens from outer space you
know."

"How d'you know?" said Molly. "They might be."

"What is it with you and statues?"

"Uh?"

"Well, if you ask me, you were pretty rude and that's not how we've
been brought up. What was with that 'whatever' thing, anyway? I've never heard you say that before?"

"Well, I was angry and I couldn't think of anything else to say."

"It was juvenile, and I thought my sister would have been smarter."

"Whatever," whispered Molly.

The two of them fell into silence.

Charlie smiled. So did Molly, and then they were both laughing.

"Seriously, what is it with you and statues?" asked Charlie. "Why do you hate them so much?"

"I don't hate them. Where'd you get that from? I don't like them. I don't see why we have them, and everything I've learned in history is that many don't deserve recognition in the first place."

"You certainly made that clear tonight."

"Yeah, well," said Molly, "I think we should get hold of Mum and Dad. There's an emergency number with the university, and they can contact them for us."

"My guess is they'll have already done that. This is serious stuff, you know. Besides, Mum and Dad have probably seen their daughter on CNN, and are heading home right now."

Molly stuck her tongue out.

"But I'll ring the uni' in the morning," said Charlie.

Molly flicked on the TV, hoping not to see her face. Every channel was showing something on the statues, some live coverage, now under lighting; history facts and discussion groups. There was a lot of emphasis on the statues ability to communicate with each other, apparently something they had been doing for centuries.

A redheaded presenter, wearing a striped shirt and a bow tie, was announcing that their network had made an approach to get the statue of William Shakespeare on tomorrow's programme. The same presenter introduced four other people in the studio and explained what each person did for a living and their speciality. There was a politician, a high-ranking member of the church, an historian and a conservationist. The first three were men, the last one a woman.

There was some discussion on the effects on London, and what the day's events actually meant. The guest speakers then theorised as to how this was happening. Later, they would be taking questions from the studio audience.

The conservationist got her say early in the programme. "Whoever they are, we need to be listening to what they are telling us," she said.

There was a brief silence.

"About saving the planet…" There was a hint of sarcasm in her voice. "This is our wake up call. You know it's quite amazing. If you stopped the average person on the street, and asked how could we reduce global warming, they'd have no problem telling you. We all know what needs to be done," the conservationist continued, turning to face the studio audience. "Are we ready to do it?"

The audience clapped, and some cheered.

The television then showed a stout man with frizzy hair standing in the audience. "The only way to explain this is that we are dealing with another life form, probably from another planet," he said.

The redheaded presenter interrupted, "We're talking aliens here?"

Molly pushed herself up from the sofa and folded her legs underneath her. She gave a quick glance at her brother to make sure he was listening.

"Yes," said the stout man.

There was a murmur around the studio.

"That's the only way to explain how they control metal and stone so that it can move. They have a technology, on a molecular level, which is beyond our comprehension."

"See," said Molly. "I'm not the only one who doubts what they are saying." The presenter put the point to the politician.

"I can't comment on them being aliens," he said, "but clearly the technology is fascinating and something we will want to study."

The presenter turned to the representative from the church.

"Reincarnation, Reverend?"

"Well, this seems to go a long way towards showing that there is life after death," said the church member. "In our creation of statues, and there will be some who say this is idolatry, we have allowed them to take shape, to have a presence. This ability to communicate with each other, a type of telepathy, perhaps. Is this not the same as prayer, only much more powerful?"

The historian raised a hand. "I think we should look to the Greeks for some answers here. The Gods created copies of themselves, as in the ancient Greeks, they in turn, created copies of the Gods, in statues. This gave pleasure to the Greeks, and delighted the Gods.

"In a way we are doing the same thing," interjected the conservationist. "Do we not create replicas of ourselves in robotics? What are those robots doing now but manufacturing more machines."

"It's more than that," replied the historian. "What is it that these statues have achieved that man has pursued without success?"

He let everyone think for a moment.

"Immortality," said the historian. "I don't think it will be long before people are having statues made in their own image, to obtain their own immortality."

"Aliens or Greek Gods?" said the presenter who then put it to an audience vote. There were a lot of 'don't knows'.

Molly wasn't a 'don't know'. Whatever they were, they weren't good.

The presenter ended the programme with, "It seems, not all of us have been ready to receive the statues with kindness and true British hospitality."

Molly appeared on television. They showed her asking the question on Mary Seacole, the crowd's response and Molly's gesture. The presenter made a derogatory comment about the youth of today. Molly's face burned as she looked between her brother and the television. She vowed to prove them wrong.

The Home Secretary and the Police Commissioner stepped out of the building. They each had a car and a driver waiting. It was just after four in the morning and they had been in an emergency planning meeting for several hours. The streets of Whitehall were empty.

"What an unbelievable day," said the Home Secretary.

"I'm still pinching myself to check that I'm not dreaming," said the Commissioner. "I'm not, am I?"

"You seemed to get on well with Churchill," said the Home Secretary. "I actually thought at one stage you were whispering private jokes to each other."

"Not at all," said the Commissioner. "He saved us before, I see him doing it again."

"It will be busier tomorrow," said the Home Secretary. "It will take much of the Public another twenty-four hours to come to terms with what is actually happening. They won't want to believe some of this, even when they see it for themselves. Can your people cope?"

"Well, I can't say we have any contingency plans for statues coming to life but we'll do the best we can. We've coped with most things that have been thrown at us."

"You'll have to. This could easily lead to mass hysteria, riots, even suicides. The end is nigh and all that sort of thing." He looked up into the night sky. "Looks like the weather is changing. Let's hope that's not an omen."

Tuesday ...

Molly was somewhere in the centre of town on a dull, overcast day. She was in a large open space, such as a park, and in the centre was an enormous red and white striped tent. A big top. It was a circus and Molly could hear circus music.

She was at an opening, a flap in the tent, and she pulled it to one side. It was heavy and had a plastic feel to it. Inside, it was dark. She ducked in through the opening, and stood for a moment to allow her eyes to become adjusted to the half-light.

The circus tent was full of clowns, hundreds of them. All had white faces and white hands. They beckoned her into the centre; smiling faces and big red noses. As she walked forward, the clowns parted, creating a pathway for her. They seemed pleased to see her.

There was a terrific roar, and Molly jumped. It was a huge lion. The lion didn't attack, but sat back on its haunches. It opened its mouth in a gigantic yawn, and Molly could now see inside the lion's mouth. It had a huge, thick tongue and big teeth, and there was stringy saliva stretching between its jaws. Its breath smelt foul.

The clowns were gesturing for Molly to step forward and to put her head into the lion's mouth. A couple of them did so to show her what to do, turning their heads sideways whilst holding onto the lion's jaws.

"No way," she said, "that's stupid."

Molly saw her parents. They too were dressed as clowns, with painted white faces and white hands. They were smiling and beckoning her to approach the lion. They wanted her to put her head into the lion's mouth.

"But Mum, Dad, it's dangerous."

There was a crack of a whip from behind her and a sudden gasp from the clowns, as sand and sawdust flicked up from the floor. The whip cracked again and the clowns recoiled. Even the lion shuffled backwards. Molly searched for her Mum and Dad but they were lost to the crowd.

Molly turned, and there in front of her, was the Ringmaster. He was a big man with big features, wearing a bright red jacket and top hat with white hair protruding at the sides. He cracked the whip again and again, skilfully missing Molly each time. After each crack of the whip, he took one step forward. The clowns were diminishing, fading in the half-light.

The Ringmaster was now standing alongside her. He was looking down at her but she couldn't quite make out his face.

"Don't you remember me?" he said.

The digits flipped over to show 07:00 and at the same time, the clock radio announced the seven o'clock news. Molly startled into wakefulness. She lay there for a moment, trying to remember the dream, and reminding herself of yesterday's events. Still in her pyjamas, she went downstairs, and found Charlie sitting in an armchair watching television. He had a dishevelled and bleary look, and he was surrounded by assorted dirty crockery and empty packets of snacks.

"Have you been up all night?" said Molly.

"Just about," said Charlie glancing momentarily from the television. "You should see some of the stuff that's going on. Some people are going to make a real killing out of all this. They've had people dressed as statues, talking with statues. Photographers taking pictures of tourists posing with statues. Lots of coverage on statues talking and explaining what it was like in their days. This collective thought they've got is really weird. It seems they all know what each other is thinking. They've done some cool tricks with statues on opposite sides of London, and the tour guide companies are already selling interactive London statue tours."

Something registered in Molly's brain. "I had a really weird dream last night, I need to tell you about it."

Charlie listened to his sister .

"That's weird, do you think you've had some kind of premonition?"

"How do you mean," said Molly.

"Well, the clowns are clearly the statues, with their white faces. I would say the lion is probably some danger, and you're having to face it even though Mum and Dad are saying it's ok. Not sure who the Ringmaster is though."

"I think I do." said Molly. "Do you remember the tour we did when we first came back here? We went round looking at all the famous places. It was my birthday. We had a guide. I think he is the Ringmaster in my dream."

"That was years ago. I can't believe you can remember what he looks like?"

"I can't. I just think he's the man in my dream. Remember he told me the statue of Nelson was watching me."

"He said that as a joke."

"I think I should contact him and see what he has to say about all this."

"You can't be serious."

Molly was.

"Look Moll. Firstly, I don't think it's a good idea to go and speak to some complete stranger, and secondly, he was old then and that was what, nine years ago. I should think he's retired by now, or even dead, how on earth are you going to find him?"

Molly leapt up and clambered upstairs. Pulling out a shoe box from under her bed, she found a large, brown envelope. It was unsealed, worn at the edges, and bulged with its contents. She tipped it out onto her bed. There was a pile of birthday cards, six candles, a ribbon from a birthday cake and a small scrapbook. Distracted by the birthday cards, she started to read some of the messages. It had been Molly's birthday and the family's first year back in England. She had been unhappy at leaving her life and friends in Guatemala, and the trip to Trafalgar Square had been a birthday treat.

Molly finally turned to the scrapbook, which had all sorts of bus tickets and pamphlets in it. Some photographs had come loose. She then found the small certificate glued into one of the pages. 'The London Guides' she read. *This is to certify that Molly Hargreaves completed the historical tour of London.* Witnessed and signed by Geoffrey Gray. Now she had his name.

Molly dropped the scrapbook down on the kitchen table in front of Charlie, opened at the certificate.

"Well, there's his name."

Charlie read the certificate. "You kept this all this time?"

"Looks like it, doesn't it. How can we get his address?"

Charlie shrugged. "Telephone directory maybe, but we don't know what area. Maybe on the internet?" He was playing with ideas. He thought for a moment then smiled. "Hand me the phone," he said, "I've a cheeky idea." He dialled the number from the bottom of the certificate.

"You sure about this?" said Charlie as he waited for an answer.

"Yes," said Molly. "Who you calling?"

"I'm going to get you the address and I'm going to be an American to do it."

"The London Guides, how may I help you?" said the voice.

Molly quickly slid onto the bench-seat next to her brother, who titled the phone so she could hear both sides of the conversation.

"How you doin'?" said Charlie in a strong deliberate American slur.

Molly screwed up her face.

"I am telephoning you from the United States of America." Charlie paused. "I was over in your pretty country a couple of years ago and I went on one of your tours."

"Yes, sir," said the woman in the office. "We trust you enjoyed it?"

"I sure did. We had a Tour Guide whose name is Geoffrey Gray."

"Ah yes," said the woman."

"I meant to give him a tip. He did such a splendid job for us but I didn't have any of your English pounds on me, so I promised to send him something. I lost his details but my wife, whilst clearing out the ga-raage this morning, found his card. So I was wondering, is he still with you?"

Molly was in hysterics, giggling through her fingers.

"Unfortunately sir, he's no longer with the company."

"That's a real shame because I have just recommended him, very highly, to a large group of friends of mine who are in London town, right now. Perhaps you could give me his address?"

"We would be happy to accommodate your friends, sir," said the woman.

"Well, that would be good, but could you just give me Mr Gray's address so that I can send him his tip?"

"Well, I'm afraid that's against company policy."

"Well, I understand that but you say he's not with the company any longer."

"I'm sorry, sir, it wouldn't be right for me to give out his address,"

"Look Ma'am, my honour as an American is at stake here. I am sure, you being British an all, can appreciate that?"

The woman was silent for a moment. "Well, I suppose Geoffrey would appreciate something, and that is very generous of you to want to send it." She gave the address and asked if Charlie wanted any of it spelt.

"Can I ask where your American friends are staying in London?" said the woman.

Charlie put the phone down.

With an exaggerated cheesy grin, Charlie swivelled the notepad towards Molly with an address in Herne Hill.

"You were brilliant," said Molly.

Molly left the house with an abundance of reassurances to her brother that she would be all right. She guessed that he would want to see Amber, and that accompanying Molly across London to find some stranger, was not part of his plans.

She had dressed conservatively, intending that she should be taken seriously. Her trousers were dark blue, almost black and she was comfortable in a high necked, blue jumper, which had vertical turquoise stripes. She didn't care much for the shoes she was wearing, as she spent most of her time in an old pair of trainers, but these ones looked smart. Her trousers didn't have a pocket for her mobile, so she took a shoulder bag that was embroidered with brightly coloured beads.

She found the Tour Guide's address easily enough, but because of the amount of people flocking to London, the journey had taken ages. During the train journey, she had tried not to think about what she was about to do, in case she backed out of it. Dark clouds were forming over London, adding to Molly's sense of foreboding.

Mr Geoffrey Gray lived on the ground floor of a block of flats next to a railway line. Before she had her last chance to change her mind, a curtain in one of the windows moved. No going back now, she thought. She gave a sharp and positive knock on the green painted door, and it was opened, immediately, by a large, overweight woman, wearing red slippers and a dirty apron that might have once been pink. She could have been somebody's aunty; kind or nasty, Molly was yet to find out.

"Excuse me for disturbing you," Molly said. "I'm looking for Mr Gray, the Tour Guide." Molly thought this last bit might allay any suspicion as to why she wanted to find Mr Gray.

"He's no here," said the woman, with a Scottish accent. She folded her arms across her chest. "And I a nae seen him."

It looked as though she was going to be mean and nasty.

"Now what does a wee lass like you want with a man like Gray? Who are youse, anyhow?" she said.

"It's about the statues," explained Molly, "I need—"

"Oh, those bloody statues,"interrupted the woman. "Well, that's where you'll find him, in the pub with a bunch of them. He's fascinated by them, he is. Spent all those years blethering on aboot them and now the damn things come to life. It's a curse, it's no natural, I can tell you."

Molly was taken aback by the outburst and it must have shown in her face.

The woman unfolded her arms and looked at Molly, perhaps appreciating that none of it was Molly's fault.

"Sorry, would ye'd like a cup of tea, my dear?"

Molly wasn't sure.

"Come on, come and have some tea and tell me what it is you want." Unexpectedly, the woman stepped out of the flat, closing the door behind her, then used a key to open the flat next door.

"I live in here, my dear," she said looking at Molly's confused expression. "Oh, did you think I was Mrs Gray?" she added with over-exaggerated laughter. "No, I'm a neighbour. I mind his hoose, cleaning and that, he's not very good at looking out for himself." She brushed Molly into the hallway with a series of flicks of a hand behind Molly's left shoulder.

Inside, the woman introduced herself as Barbara. Her manner and accent relaxed as she described how she had met Geoffrey Gray, when he moved into the block of flats.

"He had seemed all out of place. Didn't know where the local shops were, or even where to leave his rubbish. After a couple of weeks he was'nae looking at all well. "I think he was drinking," she added in a concerned voice. "He's also one for the horses."

Molly nodded.

"He had a job as a tour guide," Barbara continued, "but he tells me the company has been kind enough to offer him an early retirement. I know he wasn't happy. They started employing a lot of foreigners, he'd call them, who knew nothing about London's history."

It occurred to Molly that Mr Gray might have been sacked rather than opting for early retirement. She was beginning to wonder if she'd made the right decision in enlisting the Tour Guide's help. She changed the subject by telling Barbara about the time of her sixth birthday and Trafalgar Square.

"Typical," said Barbara, "just like him to scare a young child with his stupid stories."

"Not so stupid now," Molly pointed out.

She was pleased to be talking to Barbara. She felt relaxed and went on to explain what had happened in Temple Gardens and outside the embassy.

"You must have been quite frightened, my dear." She was turning out to be a sweet and nice aunty after all.

"Do you think Mr Gray will see me? I don't suppose he will remember me."

"Let's go and find out," said Barbara, struggling slightly to get to her feet.

They left the house and within ten minutes, were standing outside a pub on the Dulwich Road. The place was packed, and with a huge fan shaped crowd outside. Molly was both excited and apprehensive about meeting the Tour Guide again, and wondered if he would remember her after all these years. She wasn't convinced that they would even get into the pub let alone find him.

Barbara, was the solution to that, and she barrelled her way through while dragging Molly by her hand. Molly found herself treading on people's toes, and repeatedly said sorry. She wondered what damage Barbara was inflicting.

Inside, three statues were stood at the bar, surrounded by mostly men. It was difficult to get a clear view. Instead of pushing her way through to the bar, Barbara took the stairs to a mezzanine floor, which looked down on the bar and where, she explained, Gray was always to be found.

"The landlord must be pleased with this crowd," said Barbara. "It's only ten in the morning."

Crushed into a corner, and next to a balustrade overlooking the bar, Barbara found her neighbour at a table with a large glass of red wine, a cigarette and a notepad and pen. He was a big man with big features and white, unkempt hair.

Molly recognised him immediately.

Mr Gray looked surprised.

"This is Miss Molly Hargreaves," said Barbara. "You scared her half to death when she was six years old, telling her about Nelson coming alive."

"Yes, yes, I know who she is," said Gray with several impatient waves of a huge hand trying to quieten her.

Molly connected the names; Gee-Gee, the man at mum and dad's party, is Geoffrey Gray.

Barbara was staring at Gray awaiting his next response.

"So, we meet again," said Molly. She had no recollection of him from nine years ago, when he showed the family around London as a tour guide, and couldn't place him her dream as the Ringmaster.

Barbara went to sit down even though there were no empty seats, and a young man cleared his chair just in time, probably more out of self-preservation than politeness. Someone pushed a stool forward and Molly sat down as well.

"I don't understand," said Barbara.

Molly wasn't sure what to say. Gray hadn't exactly been very nice to her at the party. She found herself just staring at him.

Mr Gray was staring at Molly.

Barbara spoke again, this time lowering her voice. "Molly here, thinks that the statues are up to nay good." She glanced down at the three statues at the bar for the first time. Molly remained silent.

It was Gray who spoke. "Let me tell you about these characters in here," he said, nodding towards the three statues. "We have here, no less, the statues of George IV, Charles Fox and Beau Brummell."

Molly raised herself off her stool to get a view of them. The three statues were still standing at the bar with a crowd of people around them. Those at the front were seated and with standing room only towards the back and the entrance. Molly was transfixed. They were like people dressed as statues with an odd way of moving, slightly slow motion, slightly jerky. They were talking amongst themselves, recounting their own stories to each other, as well as answering questions from the crowd. Occasionally, they would break into raucous laughter, throwing back a head, and sometimes slapping the bar with an open hand. It was surreal.

"In real life, whatever real life is these days," continued Gray, "these three were good mates and drinking chums. George IV, who was the Prince Regent, became King, and married Caroline of Brunswick. It was an arranged marriage and before she got married, she sent him one of her teeth as a token of her affection."

Mr Gray was sounding like a Tour Guide. "He was rather over indulgent and weighed over 17 stone, with a fifty inch waist. They had a daughter together but it was an unsuccessful marriage, and George actually paid his wife to stay out of England. He enjoyed his drink and ran up enormous bills."

Barbara tutted.

"The one in the robes is Charles James Fox," he continued. "That object in his hand is the Magna Carter. He was a politician, a good one for a debate, he liked gambling, women and politics, and apparently in that order. The other well-dressed gentleman, with top hat and cane, is George Bryan Brummell, Beau to his friends. He used to wear fancy clothes, and introduced the wearing of a suit and tie. He normally stands in Jermyn Street, where all the gentleman's outfitters are. Apparently, he used to take five hours to get dressed, and polished his boots with champagne. What a waste, eh? Another with a high life and high debts."

"What's a Prince Regent?" said Molly, already fascinated by all this knowledge.

"A Prince Regent is someone who rules in the absence or incapacity of the King or Queen. In this case, he took over because his father, George III went a bit mad and couldn't cope. The father died in 1820, and George then became King. He was called Prinnie by his friends and he was responsible for the building of the Brighton Pavilion.

"Fox," Gray continued, "known as CJ, was against George III, that's the dad, and they battled over politics. He had debts, one hundred and forty-thousand pounds at one stage. He was a Dandy like Beau Brummell. Do you know what a Dandy is?"

Molly nodded, "Someone who wears fancy clothes."

"The odd thing is," Gray leaned forward and lowered his voice even further, "the statue of Prinnie is when he is King, so after 1820. However, in 1817, Beau and the Prince had a falling out when Brummell saw the Prince Regent in the street one day with a man called Alvanley. He asked Alvanley who was the fat friend he was with, referring to the Prince Regent. Brummell left to live in France where he died. Therefore, it's a bit odd to see them in here together. This is also the wrong venue."

"What do you mean?" said Molly.

"You would find them in a Gentlemen's club such as White's Club in St James's Street, and I don't doubt that they would get entry. You would not have found them in a public house, even if it is called the Prince Regent."

"Do you think they're bad?"

The Tour Guide looked surprised at the question. "As in evil?" he said.

Molly nodded.

"No, I don't think they are evil. You can always find some bad in most of our historical figures. I'm not entirely sure what they are doing here?" he added. "I've been listening to them for quite a while now, and they haven't exactly been talking about saving the planet. The three seem to be here just for a good time."

Geoffrey Gray looked down at the statues again, they were ordering more beer, and still holding the fascination of everyone in the pub. "It's been jolly interesting though, hearing about what was going on in their day. Let's get out of here where we can have a bit of a chat."

The three of them squeezed their way towards the door, their empty seats being filled immediately. Outside, the crowd of people trying to get in had grown.

"Come home with us, young lady, and have a cup of tea," said Barbara.

Molly, who didn't like tea, smiled and nodded. She was pleased to have found the Tour Guide, and she was impressed by his knowledge; he clearly knew what he was talking about.

The Police Commissioner was at New Scotland Yard and being briefed. On a large screen attached to the wall was a map of London. The current positions of living statues were shown with flashing icons, and one of his officers was reading from a briefing sheet.

"After the incident at Heathrow, the statues of Alcock and Brown are now in a secure compound and being guarded," he said. "They were found, as non-living statues, in one of the hangers on the east-side of the airport. We think they might have been trying to take a plane."

"They've not come alive again?" said the Commissioner.

"No, sir."

"Churchill has explained to the PM that the airport and St Thomas' were just glitches. Over enthusiasm on their part, an opportunity to come to life, unfinished business," said the Commissioner. "We don't need to concern ourselves."

"We have arranged for Brunel, Shakespeare and Nightingale to stay in Hyde Park," continued the briefing officer. "Crowd management has become easier there, and the Press are happy with the set up."

"Good," said the Commissioner.

"Brummell, Fox and George IV are still in the same pub," said the briefing officer. "We've plain-clothes officers in there of course. There's a large crowd of women surrounding the statue of Achilles, apparently, they're hoping he's going to come alive and remove his fig leaf."

Everyone in the room chuckled.

"Here's another nice touch," said the briefing officer. "Yesterday afternoon, in Pimlico, a JCB driver collided with a main support of a disused garage. The roof and a wall collapsed trapping a passing woman. The JCB driver didn't dare try lifting the debris, for fear of further injuries, but the statue of the Master Builder, Thomas Cubitt did."

There was a ripple of approval from around the room.

"The woman got out with cuts and bruises. The fire brigade were on scene. They said the statue's strength was phenomenal, and they would have struggled to have done it so quickly."

"Have we given that story to the Press?" said the Commissioner.

"I'm sure they've got it sir, but I'll check," said the Press Officer.

"Our main problems," continued the briefing officer, "are still with traffic and pedestrian congestion. We've implemented our road closure and circulatory systems but everyone wants to come and look. We've queues worthy of Disneyland of people wanting footage with themselves and statues. We have philosophical and historical debates going on, and where statues haven't come alive, we've got people camping out waiting in case they do."

"I'll talk to the PM about sealing the City from outside visitors, just until we get a grip of things," said the Commissioner.

"We've had some damage, statues being vandalised. A man was arrested last night in Kensington Gardens trying to destroy the statue of Peter Pan with a sledgehammer. In interview, he said that he didn't want Peter Pan coming to life and taking his children off to Neverland. We've now either a police presence or camera on nearly all our statues," continued the briefing officer. "We've taken quite a lot of calls from people who are concerned about such things as: lions coming alive at Nelson's column, gargoyles and other mythical creatures, and talking heads."

"Churchill assures us they won't and I don't think we need worry about it," said the Commissioner. He hesitated for a moment. "It might be interesting though, to discuss some what-if scenarios, and how we would deal with them. Let's start with those lions."

It didn't take long to get back to the Geoffrey Gray's flat. During the walk, he had asked Molly how she had found him and why. She told him about Charlie's telephone call, and of the contact she'd already had with the statues.

"They're not right," she said. "I can't explain it, but I feel they are up to something."

"Up to what, exactly?" said Gray. "I get the clear impression you don't like them, and as you were scared by one and embarrassed by another, one could hardly say you have conclusive evidence that they are evil."

"They've come to us with a message on conservation," started Molly.

"And one that we have known for some time but have done little about," said Gray.

"But if it was that desperate, Mum and Dad would have said something. This is what they do."

"Your parents may not know everything about the state of the planet."

"How do you know my parents?" Said Molly.

"Oh, we go back a long way. We used to work at the university together, and we've worked on the same expeditions over the years. We knew each other at uni. I may not have been in touch that often, but I've always been interested in what you and your brother have been up to."

They arrived at Gray's flat, and he put his key into his front door, but before turning it, he looked at Barbara.

"Thank you for bringing Molly to me," he said in a rather dismissive tone. Barbara looked disappointed.

"I'm right next door," she said to Molly, "if there's anything you need." She stepped into her own flat.

"Damn woman," said Gee-Gee as soon as her door had closed. He opened his own door. "She means well but does poke her nose where it's not welcome. I always feel she's spying on me."

"She's really nice," said Molly. "I think that's a bit unfair of you." Gray didn't respond.

Inside, the place was overburdened with furniture, knickknacks and clutter. Too many possessions in too small a space, was how Gray described it. Molly had considered that as Mr Gray looked so dishevelled in his appearance, that he might smell or that his flat might be dirty and unclean. She was pleased to establish that neither of these two concerns were true.

There were many books. Big, heavily bound academic type books, the sort that Molly couldn't envisage anyone having the patience to read. Leather and wooden ornaments decorated the place, showing that Mr Gray had seen the world. Molly recognised some pieces from her own travels.

"Right then, first things first, please call me Gee-Gee," said Geoffrey Gray.

"All right, Gee-Gee" said Molly. "What's an Agalmata?"

"Agalmata?" said Gee-Gee. "That's a strange question, where have you heard that name?"

"From you, at the party," said Molly.

"Really? Yes, of course," said Gee-Gee. "Agalmata is the collective word the ancient Greeks gave to their statues and other objects of art." He selected an ornament from a shelf. It was a carved wooden head from Tanzania. "This head is meaningless to you. A nice piece of art but nothing more. If, however, you had been brought up to believe it was sacred, magical, of great value, you might hold it in higher esteem or even worship it. It would take on a special meaning, a deity. That's what the Greeks called Agalmata."

"So Agalmata is piece of art or a statue?"

"A piece of art or a statue that is special, in some way."

Molly nodded. That seemed clear enough, but he hadn't used Agalmata in that context when he mentioned it at her parents' party. She couldn't remember his exact words, but it wasn't to do with ancient Greeks. She watched him as he replaced the carved head.

"So, young Molly," said Gee-Gee. "What's your plan?"

Molly looked blank. "I'm not sure I've got one. I just think that something is wrong with the whole situation, and I don't believe they are here to save us. I don't know why, just a feeling."

"Now you're not saying this because you want to be famous?"

"But, I don't—"

Gee-Gee was smiling. "I'm joking, and I was a little unfair to you at the party. I suppose what we need is something to prove your feelings are right — or wrong, of course. How about this? We ask them, in a roundabout way—"

"Ask them?" said Molly.

"Yes, we could put questions to them, and see if they all come up with the same answers. For example, are they who they say they are? If we ask them questions about themselves and the times they lived in, we would know if it was George IV or Will Shakespeare."

"A sort of interrogation?"

"Sort of. We could ask them about conservation, about saving the planet, as that's their reason for being here."

"I could do that," said Molly.

"And finally we could look for anything that's odd or out of the ordinary?" said Gee-Gee.

"What? You mean apart from walking, talking, living statues on the streets of London?"

They both smiled.

"If they are working to some sort of agenda, there may be times when it's not going according to plan. If we know that, we should be able to spot any weaknesses."

Molly liked the questions. "When do we start?" she asked.

"Now, if you want. I don't think there's any point in going back to the pub. We know what they are doing. I've someone in mind that will fit the bill exactly. He's a bit out of the way but that should mean there won't be any crowds. Let's grab a cab and I'll brief you on the way."

There was a briefing on the hour, every hour in COBR. In a short period, the adjoining rooms had become operational. Telephones were busy with a bank of operators recording information and inputting this to computers. The information was also displayed on large screens around the room with electronic maps showing what was going on. In Churchill's day, they would have pushed numbered wooden blocks around a tabled map, using long poles; today things were a lot more high tech. The statue of Churchill put his hands on his hips and surveyed the room.

"What do you think?" said the Prime Minister.

"Impressive, Prime Minister, very impressive. Of course, we may have come from the past, but we haven't stood still with our communications. I'm referring of course to our ability to talk to each other."

The Prime Minister nodded. "Do you know how it works?"

"Not really," said Churchill. "But it is something we have been doing for a long time. It feels as though we are all in the same room together, a darkened room, where we can speak but not see each other. It is most peculiar."

"A type of E.S.P?"

"An extrasensory perception — perhaps? By way of example, your cameras looking over Parliament Square will show you the amount of traffic, and what those demonstrators in front of Parliament are doing with their banners and flags. Standing here, I am able to speak freely with Disraeli, Derby, Palmerston, Peel, and Smuts." Churchill fanned an open hand through the air as if pointing to the statues in Parliament Square.

"And another one of you, of course," said the P.M. "I've been meaning to ask, what happens when there is more than one statue of the same person?"

"It appears we can only occupy one form at a time," said Churchill. "Just as well, really, can you imagine two of me making decisions?" he laughed.

Not at the rate you're drinking my booze, thought the Prime Minister.

"Let us discuss what we might expect today," said Churchill. "We've still got Nightingale, Brunel and Shakespeare doing their bit in Hyde Park. Did you know they've asked Shakespeare to appear on a TV chat show? He'll love all that. I've tasked Faraday, Myddelton and Jenner to look at something for me this morning."

The PM nodded in acceptance despite the fact that he expected to be consulted before decisions were made. He was the Prime Minister, after all.

"I've authorised any London statue to come to life, when they see the need to," continued Churchill. "I'm sure that there will be many questions, not just on the situation but also from each individual's past, their place in history. I've said they can come alive and engage in conversation but without wandering around, I thought that might be easier to police with crowds and traffic."

"That seems fine," said the Prime Minister, not entirely sure how that would work. "I have arranged a series of meetings this morning," said the PM. "We have some scientists, conservationists and eminent people who would like to meet you and discuss the future. We can work through lunch, as time is short."

The Prime Minister was escorting Churchill out of COBR as he spoke.

"Yes, I think I can fit that in, Prime Minister. We should be getting on with the situation at hand."

Once out of the room and down the corridor, the Prime Minister made an excuse of having forgotten something back in the Operations Room.

"I'll be two minutes, keep walking, Sir Winston, I'll catch up."

The Prime Minister sprinted back to the Ops Room. He shouted at one of the aids who was just about to clear up after the two guests.

"Don't touch that glass."

Everyone in the room looked round.

"Ring New Scotland Yard and get a forensic team down here," instructed the PM. "I want them to see if they can get any fingerprints from Churchill's glass. Then get them to look for DNA from this cigar butt. Contact GCHQ. I want them to see if they can pick up any trace of this ESP or other communications between statues." He hesitated for a moment. "Ask them if they think the statues can pick up what we are thinking? And, not a word to anyone."

The aid nodded in understanding, and the PM ran out to rejoin Churchill and their working lunch.

The black cab dropped Molly and Gee-Gee outside the Limehouse Library, in Tower Hamlets. Molly had just enough cash on her to pay for the fare; Gee-Gee said he had forgotten his wallet.

The grey, stone building looked sad and run down with wooden boarding over every window. Gee-Gee explained that it had fallen into disrepair and there were no immediate plans to do anything with it.

Molly spotted the statue. Its head was turned to one side and one hand holding the lapel of its jacket. She felt a little uneasy as they walked through the gate into the library grounds. There was no one else around.

Gee-Gee walked up to the statue, and stood in front of it with his hands cupped behind his back. He addressed the statue in a respectful tone.

"Excuse me, sir, I wonder if we could have a moment of your time?" The statue showed no life.

"My name is Geoffrey Gray, and this is Miss Molly Hargreaves. We would like to ask you a few questions. I used to be a tour guide with a well known company here in London, and have always been interested in history".

Still no response.

Gee-Gee addressed Molly. "Did you know, Molly, this man was the Deputy Prime Minister during the war? He became Prime Minister in 1945, convincingly beating Winston Churchill." Gee-Gee's voice was full of admiration.

Molly was puzzled. Gee-Gee had told her all this on the journey over.

"He served at Gallipoli during the First World War, was seriously wounded at El Hanna, and returned to England to recover. He was then sent to fight on the Western Front in 1918, when he returned to teach at the London School of Economics.

This isn't going to work, thought Molly, maybe it's not meant to come alive. She nodded, as though interested.

"While on a trip to France, Mr Atlee met Violet Millar who later became his devoted wife."

The head turned, slowly and stiffly, and with an irritating grating noise. Immediately, Molly felt a little nauseous and had a strong desire to run. Gee-Gee took hold of her arm as the statue stared down on them.

"Good morning to you, sir," said Gee-Gee, looking pleased with himself. The statue said nothing. "We do hope we are not disturbing you?"

The statue opened its mouth to speak. Nothing happened at first, as if it had forgotten how to speak; then the voice was rasping.

"I met Violet, in Italy, not France."

That was Gee-Gee's first test on whether the statue was the real thing.

"Did you know that you were recently voted as the best Prime Minister of the 20th century?" said Gee-Gee.

"Really," said the statue.

"You are shown as having been a loyal ally of Winston Churchill during the war."

"That is true," said the statue.

"I just wondered, why Churchill was now in Parliament advising the current Prime Minister as to the state of affairs, while you are standing out here, on this cloudy, miserable day, in front of this disused library?"

This was Gee-Gee's next test question; to see if there was any other agenda amongst the statues.

"We all have our place," said the statue of Atlee.

"That's very modest of you, and wasn't it Churchill who said that you were a modest man, but then you had so much to be modest about?"

The statue looked puzzled.

"I believe you were in disagreement with Churchill over rearming after the First World War.

"I'm not sure what your point is?"

"I'm just curious as to your role in this whole thing?"

"I don't have a role. This world is in trouble. Not just because of the things that you have done, but because of all of us. We have failed to understand the complexity of the planet and the need to maintain a balance; the status quo between all living things. The past has come to life to help change that. Life, if you like, is trying to sustain itself.

"If we are talking conservation…" Gee-Gee looked at Molly, it was her time to ask one of the questions that Gee-Gee had prepared for her.

Molly's mind went blank. She had been so absorbed by the conversation that she had completely forgotten that she had a part in all of this. There was an awful silence.

Gee-Gee broke it. "I find it interesting that it was your government who decided that Britain should have an independent atomic weapons programme. You will be aware no doubt, that today we have wars to prevent countries from obtaining their own nuclear weapons. How does that stand with conserving the planet?"

"It is easy to look with hindsight as to the decisions we made, and to judge them," said the statue. "The point is, action is needed now, and that action needs to be radical."

There's definitely a party line here between the statues and the need to save the planet, decided Molly, feeling relieved that Gee-Gee had taken over the interrogation.

Gee-Gee and Clement Atlee bantered on together about a number of subjects, all of which were fascinating to Molly. She was enthralled by Gee-Gee's knowledge on history, and how easily he had engaged the statue.

After a while, Gee-Gee thanked Mr Atlee for his time and patience and hoped his questions had all been taken in good humour. The statue had already returned to being a lifeless object.

Molly followed Gee-Gee out on to Commercial Road, where Gee-Gee looked for another black cab. They headed into the City.

"You were just brilliant," said Molly.

"I'm so sorry about my part. I just got tongue tied and didn't know what to say."

"You would never have made a politician," said Gee-Gee. "You'll do better at the next one," he said, smiling. He was obviously enjoying this.

"I'm not entirely sure what we got out of interviewing Mr Atlee," said

Gee-Gee. "He was a brilliant Prime Minister. He brought in a lot of social reform straight after the war and at a time when the country really needed it. His government had a role in the National Health system and the creation of the National Parks. He served this country well."

Molly reflected on the things she was learning on this trip.

"He was spot on with his facts about his own life," Gee-Gee continued, "showing, I suppose, that he is who he says he is. He remained consistent with what we have heard from other statues concerning the state of the planet, and he didn't get fazed when I asked him some more personal questions, which is exactly what you would expect from Clement Richard Atlee."

"Where to now?" said Molly.

One of the things discussed over lunch, was what was happening to the food and drink that Churchill was consuming, if consuming was the right word to use.

"I haven't the slightest idea," said Sir Winston.

"Can you taste it?" was the next question from one of the ministers.

"Only too well. Don't ask me how, gentlemen but believe me, after all these years, it tastes bloody good."

The ministers showed their approval.

"Let's talk conservation," Churchill said to the Prime Minister and anyone else who cared to listen. "There's no easy fix. It's going to take determination and effort. I know the Americans haven't exactly been playing ball, and I may be able to help out there, but you, Prime Minister, must lead the way."

"What exactly do I need to do?" said the PM.

Churchill pondered for a moment. "If I said, take all vehicles off the road, tomorrow, accepting that you would need to make exception with essential and emergency transportation, would you do it?"

The Prime Minister pulled at his right earlobe. "If you are telling me that's what it's going to take. I'd do it."

"Then that's the plan," said Churchill, slapping a hand down onto the table. "Make the order this afternoon."

The Prime Minister looked horrified. How could he possibly order, let alone enforce, no vehicular traffic on British roads? How would people get to work? How would things be delivered? How would his wife get the kids to school?

"I can see you don't like that idea," said Churchill. "How about grounding all aircraft then, they must be warming up the atmosphere with the amount of carbon they are pumping out?"

The Prime Minister considered that for a moment: the airlines, their employees, businessmen, holidaymakers, supermarket food. The list would be endless. They'd have him ousted from government within the week.

Churchill looked serious, as he puffed at his cigar. "It's going to need something like that. The world needs a rethink on how you go about your daily lives, and you need to act together. Whether it's transport, industry or power, you need to get on with it. Think of it this way. If you were at war, what lengths would you go to in order to win? Financially, economically, what would you ask of the people during this war and what would they be prepared to give? As we did, not so very long ago. I suggest you would do whatever it takes. That is what you need to do now, Prime Minister."

The Prime Minister curled back into his chair with deep concern. He knew his Cabinet were watching him. All this had fallen on his shoulders, a huge responsibility. He took a long gulp from his cognac glass.

Molly had to dissuade Gee-Gee from going to a pub. He had said that it would be a good place to think about where to go next. Instead, they were now on the Central Line heading for Chancery Lane.

"We'll go to my namesake instead," said Gee-Gee. "Gray's Inn."

Molly glared at him.

"No, it is not a pub," said Gee-Gee laughing. "They are legal buildings. All barristers have to belong to one of four Inns in London. Some of them live there, along with judges and other clever people."

"Why are we going there?"

"To see Sir Francis Bacon."

During the journey, at Molly's request, Gee-Gee talked about some of his interests and the places he had been to.

"Do you live on your own?" said Molly.

"Yes, I do," said Gee-Gee.

"No wife, no girlfriend?"

"No, no wife, no girlfriend, I'm quite happy on my own. My life has always been busy and I cope well, just me."

"It's just Barbara mentioned when you first moved in—"

"See what I mean about that woman?"

"But she cleans for you, and it seems to me she does a good job."

"I get her to clean as she needs the money. I could do it just as well myself, maybe I should."

Molly was curious of the relationship between Barbara and Gee-Gee, but felt she had asked enough. She changed the subject. "My dad said that you're very clever and an authority on history."

"My word that is high acclaim indeed. I'm not sure one can say I am an authority on history. Certain parts of history, maybe, but not all of it. Do you like history?"

"Yes, I do. I do a lot of reading, and history is one of my favourite subjects. I'm home schooled."

"I know. When you were younger, your parents talked about me being involved in some of your education. I used to have a lot of contact with your parents. We used to work together. In fact, I am a sort of unofficial godfather to both you and your brother."

Molly was surprised.

"You were never christened so it was just a family thing, but I lost contact with your mum and dad."

"I never knew that."

"They never told you? It's not important."

Molly thought for a moment about what it meant to have a godfather. Gee-Gee was certainly an odd character but he seemed sincere. She studied his face. She'd noticed his habit of brushing his hair back with a hand only to have if fall forward again.

"My dad said you lost your job one time," she said, trying to get to know more about him. "Was that why you were working as a tour guide?"

"You know your father has done well for himself, he has a lot of ability, but he could be achieving more. I hope you are going to do something special with your life. Ah, this is our stop," he said, moving closer to the doors.

Molly and Gee-Gee jogged up the steps from the platform. She was pleased to be back in the open. They walked into Gray's Inn Road and then turned left into a service road that led into Gray's Inn, a huge complex of buildings surrounded by a high wall. At the end of the service road, was a small wooden white painted booth and a barrier, controlling traffic entering and leaving the complex. There was a man inside the wooden booth, and as they approached, Gee-Gee whispered to Molly that he would do the talking.

"Awright mate?" said Gee-Gee, putting on a cockney accent.

"Awright," said the man in the booth.

"We'd like to see the statue of Sir Francis Bacon, if that's ok?"

"He's gorn mate. Destroyed, ruined, some bugger come in and smashed him to pieces. Dreadful innit?"

Gee-Gee looked shocked.

"Nah," said the man, "I'm joking, he's still 'ere. There's no sign of him being alive and kicking though."

Gee-Gee gave a half-hearted laugh. "You had me going. Nice one, mate. What's yah name?"

The man introduced himself as Danny.

"He's through that archway," said Danny. "First courtyard and he's on the right 'and side."

"Awright. Can we go and see him?" asked Gee-Gee. "I know we ain't got no appointment," he joked.

"I'm not suppose' to let anyone in," said Danny. Then he added, "he had a bit of chequered past, you know. Clever bloke, but did you know, right, he wrote some of Shakespeare's plays for him? He was a judge, right, but he got caught taking a bribe, and ended up in the Tower of London."

Molly decided that Danny told all visitors to Bacon's statue these details. Like Gee-Gee, he probably knew a lot about history. Molly could see how the two of them would get on well together.

"We've had to close the courtyard, since the statues come alive," said Danny. "Just in case someone does come in and damage him. But listen, just you two slope in there, and you'll see him on the right."

Gee-Gee thanked Danny, winked at Molly and led her under the archway. "It's all about how you speak to people," said Gee-Gee.

They walked into a big open courtyard surrounded by high, red-bricked buildings. The place looked neat and tidy. The statue was at one end of a trimmed lawn that was surrounded by expensive-looking parked cars.

Sir Francis Bacon was dressed in heavy garments and holding an equally heavy-looking book. In the other hand was a cane, and around his neck was one of those frilly things known as a ruff. It was common in his time, but it looked uncomfortable.

Gee-Gee turned to Molly. "I think it best if I have a chat with this statue alone. Do you mind just waiting here while I'll see if I can get some information out of him?"

Trusting Gee-Gee's judgement, Molly waited near the archway.

The statue came to life immediately and climbed down off his plinth, and shook hands with Gee-Gee. Molly could hear them talking, but couldn't make out what was being said. She watched, as the statue appeared to be explaining something. It was a peculiar scene and very different to the encounter with the statue of Clement Atlee. Gee-Gee looked unsettled, as if he was being told something he didn't want to hear, and occasionally glanced in Molly's direction. The statue wagged a finger at him, and a couple of times actually poked Gee-Gee in the chest. Then, both statue and Gee-Gee turned and looked straight at Molly, just for a moment, then back at each other, and carried on with their conversation.

Danny appeared next to Molly. "Blimey," he said, "he got him to come alive."

He wasn't the only one to have noticed. Several windows around the courtyard had opened with people leaning out. Some people had left their offices, and were beginning to gather in and around the square.

Gee-Gee and Bacon seemed to suddenly notice that their conversation was drawing a crowd. Their voices dropped and Bacon seemed to be giving some final instructions. He was the one talking, and Gee-Gee was nodding.

"What do you fink's going on?" said Danny.

"I don't know," said Molly. "I was told to wait here."

Then, without any formal goodbyes, Sir Francis Bacon hauled himself back up onto his plinth, and instantly turned back into its rigid form.

"What was that all about," said Molly, as Gee-Gee reached the archway.

"Nothing much," said Gee-Gee, acting if nothing had happened. "We were debating the three things that have most changed the world. He believes it was printing, gunpowder and the compass."

"Did you give him a run for his money?" said Danny.

"I should say so," said Gee-Gee.

They all shook hands, said their goodbyes, and Molly followed Gee-Gee back out onto Gray's Inn Road.

"I don't know what that was all about," said Molly, intending to get some answers, "but it wasn't printing, gunpowder and compasses."

Gee-Gee looked troubled. He hailed a cab, ignoring her comment. "We have to go to see another statue, in the Victoria Tower Gardens, that's next to the Houses of Parliament. We'll go by taxi."

"I'm not sure I have enough money left," said Molly.

"That's ok, I've found some. I'll pay," said Gee-Gee.

The statue of Sherlock Holmes duly appeared at the entrance to New Scotland Yard. No one was expecting him, but they were not that surprised by his visit. His arrival quickly created a buzz throughout the entire building. After setting off all the metal detectors and stating quite honestly, he had nothing in his pockets, he was allowed into the building. There was some concern at first, as to whether the floors could cope with his weight but the building had been built to deal with all types of eventualities. It was considered wise, however, to avoid the lifts.

A Chief Inspector was appointed as Holmes' guide through the building, most of it being offices. Holmes was shown the Operations Room and some of the security systems that cover London including the comprehensive closed circuit TV. For reasons best known to himself, but not lost on some avid fans, the statue declined to visit the secure area of seized drugs.

He was keen to visit the Criminal Investigation Department, and he stepped into the CID office to tremendous applause. As detectives stood in their ovation, Sherlock Holmes waved a nonchalant hand in recognition, and then waited for the noise to die down, before speaking.

"Thank you gentlemen, and ladies, of course," he added, with a nod of his head in their direction. "It gives me great pleasure to have this, rather singular experience of being here with you today. Over the years, my relationship with Scotland Yard has been mixed, but always interesting."

There were smiles and a few laughs around the room.

"If there are any intriguing cases," continued Holmes, "that I might offer assistance on, I would be only too pleased to have a look at them."

Anticipating such an offer, several officers had already formed a disorderly queue with case papers in their hands. It wasn't long before Holmes was lost in a sea of criminal files, forensic reports, and detectives eager to reduce their caseloads.

The cab was stuck in traffic. Gee-Gee seemed to be mesmerised by the automatic lock on the cab door, the little red light flicking on and off as the cab stopped and started.

"Talk to me, Gee-Gee," said Molly. "What did Francis Bacon say to you?"

Gee-Gee turned to face her. He looked dreadful, as if in terrible trouble, and with something to say, but just couldn't. He turned back to stare out of the window.

"Molly, think of all the books and films you've watched, where there's a secret society working behind the scenes. You might become part of it because it seems interesting, but then they want you to do certain things that you might disagree with. Whenever you try to get away from them, they always catch up with you. Whatever you do, wherever you go, the secret society is always one step ahead."

Molly remained silent.

"Has it occurred to you that the statues would have needed help?" he continued, turning his head again to look at her.

"What sort of help?"

"They've known for centuries that this would happen, that the statues would come to life; not the actual day, but that it would."

"Who has? Gee-Gee, you're not making sense."

"Who do you think has approved so many statues being built in London?" The black cab swerved into the side of the road. "I never realised how powerful they are."

"Who, Gee-Gee? Who is so powerful?"

Gee-Gee leaned forward as the vehicle was braking. "They call themselves the Agalmata."

Molly was ushered out onto the pavement as Gee-Gee thrust some money through to the driver, complaining at the same time at the cost of the journey.

"It's these flipping statues, mate," said the taxi driver. "You can't get anywhere in a hurry since they come alive."

They had stopped at one of the entrances to Victoria Tower Gardens, and Molly had a thousand and one questions to ask, but there in front of her was the statue of Emmeline Pankhurst.

Gee-Gee walked up to the base of the plinth.

There weren't many people in the park; it had started to rain and people were hiding under umbrellas, heading for shelter. Gee-Gee glanced around him, and looked a little uncomfortable at what he was about to do. He spoke to the statue, introducing himself.

The statue replied immediately. "I know who you are," she said. "Now help me down off here."

The statue managed to climb down even with Gee-Gee's ineffective attempt to help a descending bronze statue, weighing several tons. Once on the ground, Emmeline Pankhurst turned to look at Molly.

"And who might we have here then?"

Gee-Gee introduced Molly.

"Well, run along, child, while I discuss something with this man. There are some swings and a slide at the end of the park."

Molly was taken aback. She looked at Gee-Gee expecting him to say something.

Gee-Gee gave a quick false smile but said nothing. He seemed powerless.

Molly walked further into the park. She didn't understand what was so secret all of a sudden. She didn't get far when she spotted a group of statues all standing together. Not wishing to go near them, she stopped and pretended to look at the Houses of Parliament situated at the edge of the park. She felt exposed out in the open, just hanging about doing nothing.

Glancing back, Molly could see Gee-Gee and Mrs Pankhurst kneeling down over a patch of ground. They appeared to be working something out, drawing in the wet gravel. The statue caught Molly watching them and straightened up with a glare. Molly turned away and sauntered on, now towards the group of statues.

There were six of them. They looked dreadful. Sad and in pain, one man had a hand twisted upwards into the air as if in agony, the muscles and sinews on his neck were extended in detail. She read the stone plinth: *The Burghers of Calais*. All the statues were dressed in rags, and some had rope around their necks. The raindrops had beaded onto the surface of the bronze making them seem even more pitiful. One man, with a deeply down-turned mouth, was holding an enormous key.

That man spoke. "What do you think?"

The voice made Molly jump.

"About us," said the statue. "What do you think? We were created by Auguste Rodin. I think it's a good work. He intended us to be on the ground, at the same level as you, but they put us on this plinth. Shame really."

"What's a Burgher?" said Molly, getting over the sudden surprise.

"It's another word for citizen," said the statue.

"Why do you all look so unhappy?"

"We think we are walking to our death. It's 1347, and the King of England, Edward III, is besieging Calais. He has been starving us. The six of us have come forward, and agreed to give up our lives if he spares the rest of Calais. He has agreed but has insisted that we come out in rags, with nooses around our necks and the keys to the City." The statue held up the key he was holding.

"So you are all killed?"

"No, by some miracle he lets us live. Apparently, his wife Queen Philippa, who was pregnant at the time, persuades him not to kill us. She said it would be a bad omen, what with the new baby."

"That was lucky," was all that Molly could think of saying.

"Why's your friend talking to that statue?" The statue with the key nodded in the direction of Pankhurst.

"He's asking her about saving the planet." In truth, Molly had no idea what they were talking about.

"Why would she know anything about that?"

"I thought that was the message of you all?"

"She spent a lot of her life starting riots and doing damage," said the statue. "We were purposefully starved, she chose to starve herself during all her hunger strikes."

One of the other six moved. "You shouldn't be talking like that."

All the Burghers were now moving, getting down off the plinth, and in an instant, Molly found herself surrounded by them.

"What are you doing," she said, trying to back away. She looked over towards Gee-Gee to see if he had seen what was going on. There was no sign of him or Pankhurst.

"We're so hungry," wailed one of the statues, with his head in his hands. "Why should we sacrifice ourselves," moaned another.

The statues were moving around Molly, including the man with the key. Some pulled at the rope around their necks, others dragged their feet.

"We've had no food for a year."

"Even the King of France won't save us."

"We are all so weak, we can't take any more."

The wailing got worse. Some of the statues bumped into Molly causing her to stumble and spin.

"Please," pleaded Molly, "leave me alone. I haven't done anything to you." The pushing and jostling got worse. Molly couldn't see a way out. She pushed against one of the statues, with both her arms outstretched, but they didn't move. She could feel the solid strength in their bodies as the her space became smaller. She could easily be crushed between statues. She tried to calm herself, to focus.

Then, there was a gap.

Molly took it and ran.

She ran across the grass and out through an exit, which wasn't the one that she and Gee-Gee had entered. She ran straight across the road without looking. A car screeched and a motorbike swerved but both missed her.

Calm down, Molly.

She slowed to a jog and looked back to see if the statues were following. It was all clear, but she kept on jogging anyway. Crossing over Great Smith Street, she turned left, then a right, followed by a left and right again; just to make sure she wasn't being followed. She needed the police.

From Victoria Street and into Broadway, Molly found exactly what she was looking for. She ran up to the police officer. He looked as though he was guarding an entrance to a huge building with lots of mirrored-glass windows.

"I've just been chased by a statue." Molly panted the words out.

The police officer, with a gun across his chest, first looked at her and then around her at the street behind.

"Looks like the statue gave up," he said.

Molly looked back but already knew she was no longer being chased. "No, you don't understand, I was in Victoria Tower Gardens when the

Burghers of Calais came alive and attacked me. The statues are evil." She regretted using the word evil the second she said it. "I need to speak to someone, to report a crime."

"This is New Scotland Yard," said the officer pointing towards a rotating sign that said so.

Molly noted the concrete security blocks, cameras and bulletproof glass. "You can't report a crime here," said the officer. "This is not a police station. You'll have to go to the nick at Belgravia." He started to give her directions.

"No, don't you see? I'm in danger. I need to come in and talk to someone about what's going on with the statues."

The officer adopted a more patronising tone. "Look, Miss…"

"It's a simple matter of elimination," said Sherlock Holmes, still surrounded by detectives and their paperwork. "Once you eliminate all other factors, the one that remains must be the truth, no matter how unlikely that seems."

His audience nodded in agreement, but thought, in reality, it was never that easy.

Holmes wavered for a moment as if collecting a thought. He turned to the Chief Inspector. "Inspector, there's a young lady downstairs trying to enter this establishment. Might I suggest, it would be a good idea to let her in, so that she may speak to you?"

The Chief Inspector looked puzzled as to how Holmes knew this, but he picked up the phone and gave instructions.

"Well, that's it, little girl, you can stand there all you want but this is not a police station and you're not coming in." The officer had lost all patience with Molly's defiance. Another constable appeared from inside the building, and whispered in his colleague's ear. The first officer's shoulders dropped at the message, and Molly was shown into the building.

Inside, she was searched by a woman officer and her bag was emptied onto a desk. Molly realised how bedraggled she looked. Her hair was wet from the rain; her trousers felt uncomfortable against her legs. Even so, she didn't appreciate this treatment, as her mobile phone, and the contents of her bag were seized. The woman officer explained that it would all be returned when she left. Molly was given a visitors badge and her name and address recorded. She was shown into a small room, which had a table and two chairs, all of which were bolted to the floor.

Another police officer walked in. He had three stars on the epaulettes on his shoulders, and introduced himself as a Chief Inspector. The man had a podgy face and was a bit overweight.

Molly decided he worked in an office.

The Chief Inspector asked her if she needed a cup of tea, and out of politeness, she said yes.

"I understand that you claim to have been chased by a statue," said the Chief Inspector. "Why don't you tell me all about it?"

"I don't claim to have been chased, I was," said Molly. She gave an account of what had occurred in the last few hours, emphasising that she had been threatened and could have been harmed.

The Chief Inspector asked her about her parents and where she lived, and Molly explained why they weren't in the country and what they did for a living.

"I've always wanted to go to somewhere exciting like that," said the Chief Inspector. "The wife and I tend to spend our holidays sitting on a beach."

"This isn't about where to go on holiday," said Molly in frustration.

The door handle rattled as though someone was having difficulty in opening it. They both stared at the door. Molly guessed it was the tea arriving, the person struggling with two cups and the door handle. She stood up to lend a hand just as the door finally opened.

In stepped the statue of Sherlock Holmes, ducking down as he did so. Molly gasped and dropped back into her seat. The statues, here already? Molly's nightmare was continuing.

"Perhaps I might be of some assistance?" said Holmes, who hadn't arrived to bring tea.

"Ah, yes, Sherlock Holmes is here helping us with the policing operation," said the Chief Inspector. "This girl seems to be worried about the presence of the statues, and believes you are here for more sinister reasons than you claim." The Chief Inspector smirked.

"My dear fellow," said Holmes, "one should not dismiss the young lady's claims and allegations so lightly. The events as she sees them are inexplicable, and things that appear inexplicable will always warrant further investigation. What is your name, my dear?"

Molly could feel her heart pounding in her ears; she felt trapped, and tried to shrink further into her chair.

"Why do you want my name?" she said in a squeaky voice.

"Her name is Molly Hargreaves, and she lives at Hampstead Heath," volunteered the Chief Inspector.

Molly bit her lip. Great, thanks for the support, now he has my name and address.

"And you fear what exactly?" said Holmes.

"I don't fear anything, exactly," said Molly trying to regain her confidence.

"She believes the statues are out to get us," the Chief Inspector mocked. "We're all going to be decimated." He smiled at Molly.

Molly regained herself. "Actually," said Molly, "decimate, from the Latin decimus, refers to killing every tenth person, originally a punishment used in Roman times for dealing with mutinous legions."

Sherlock Holmes smiled.

"I don't believe what we are being told about the end of the planet," said Molly. "I agree there is a need to change the way things are done. Yes, we are polluting the planet, cutting down rainforests that not only use up the carbon dioxide but also store it for us, but I don't believe that we haven't got long left before the planet comes to an end." Molly was feeling better; she was on a subject that she knew something about.

"Then we seem to be in agreement," said Holmes. "The world is in danger. We need to do something about it. That's why we are here."

The room fell silent. It was clearly Molly's turn to speak.

"I rather think this is the result of an over productive imagination," said Holmes, filling in the silence.

"How can you say that?" demanded Molly. "You know nothing about me."

"On the contrary," Holmes said, pausing as if studying her. "I notice that you are not interested in fashion, as are most young ladies of your age. This shows either ignorance of such things or more likely an independence to be yourself. That seems to be supported by the way you behave and talk to your elders. You are reasonably well spoken and articulate, and there is a hint of an accent, I suspect Spanish, but not from Spain. I would say you have spent some time in South America, probably your formative years otherwise the accent would be stronger. Your shoulder bag, with the woven coloured beads, is commonly made by the women folk in Peru.

"The jewellery you are wearing is reminiscent of Amber, again from the Amazon rainforests although I reserve judgement without a further examination. You appear to be knowledgeable on conservation matters yet you are not at school, as you should be at this time of the day. That leads me to think that your lifestyle is different to most, probably privately tutored. The reasons for that maybe many, but you have ventured here without any parental support, I wonder if your parents are currently indisposed. I would surmise they are involved in the sciences, probably conservation." Sherlock Holmes delivered all this in a dogmatic tone, and it was obvious he was not searching for confirmation of his findings.

The Chief Inspector threw Molly a look as if asking, is he right.

Molly stood up. "I'm clearly wasting your time," she said, and headed for the door.

The Chief Inspector and Holmes allowed her to walk out and then followed. Back at the reception, the Chief Inspector strode off to fetch Molly's mobile phone and other possessions. Molly turned to look at the statue, who was watching the Chief Inspector.

"You would have made a good Baker Street Irregular," said Holmes without looking at her. "If you know who they were?"

Molly took his statement to be a compliment.

The statue turned to face Molly.

"Molly, I don't know how much time I have, by rights I shouldn't be here." His tone was serious. "If the other statues found out I was existing, well, they would stop us." The statue gave a furtive look into the corridor behind them.

"I have something of the utmost importance to tell you but I cannot speak here. If you dare, meet me at the Lion on Westminster Bridge in exactly one hour."

Molly stared back at him, waiting for more of an explanation.

The statue had now turned towards the Chief Inspector who was walking towards them.

"What do you mean, by rights you shouldn't be here?" she said.

"I was the master of disguise, you know," said the statue quietly while still looking in the direction of the approaching Chief Inspector.

"What disguise are you in now?" said Molly.

The statue glanced at her again. "The disguise of having once lived! Ah, here's the Chief Inspector with your things."

Molly signed for her possessions, and the Chief Inspector thanked her for coming in, and told her that she should not worry. At the door, Molly turned and stared at Sherlock Holmes. She could clearly see all the lines made by the sculptor who had created him, but the statue was showing no emotion; he was giving nothing away.

Molly stuck out her hand. "Good bye," she said.

Holmes looked disarmed but reached down and shook hands. His grip was cool but gentle. The Chief Inspector followed suit then showed her through the security door and onto the pavement.

Well, what was that all about? She brought her hand up to her nose to sniff it, expecting it to smell as if she had been handling copper change. It didn't, it was just black with London grime. She wondered if that was from the statue of Sherlock Holmes or the Chief Inspector.

The rain had stopped. Molly drifted from one street to the next, thinking through what had happened to her and this city during the last twenty-four hours. At times, it was too bewildering to grasp and yet, the more contact she had with the statues, the more normal it felt. As for this encounter with Sherlock Holmes, she had no idea. There was something about his manner that she had warmed to, even though his first appearance in the room had startled her. The statue was different from many of the others. He was tall and slim and in a bronze that was not unattractive. She had been impressed when he gave her his observations, all of which had been correct. Maybe that was it, she liked the things he had said about her.

She had worked out what the statue had meant about being the master of disguise. Of all the statues that had come to life, he was the odd one out. He had never lived. He was fictional, a creation of Sir Arthur Conan Doyle. So how did that sit with the reincarnation everyone was talking about?

Molly had never read any of the Sherlock Holmes books although she knew of the character. She had however, read about Conan Doyle. She knew that he had become interested in spiritualism and had tried to establish contact with the dead. Perhaps he had sent Sherlock Holmes on his behalf, especially as there's no statue of Conan Doyle. Sherlock Holmes had also said that if the statues knew about him, they would stop, us. Who was the us? Did that include Molly, surely not? Was it Conan Doyle? What was it that Conan Doyle and Holmes were going to do that the other statues would stop if they knew?

She reached St James's Park and walked up towards the lake. There was a crowd of people listening to a man standing on a wooden box, he was much taller than his audience. He was holding a bible above his head.

"These are God's words," he said, thrusting the book several times into the air. "Exodus 20, verse 4, never make carved idols or statues, not of anything, not any creature from the land, sea or sky."

Molly stopped just back from the edge of the crowd.

"These statues are false," continued the man. "We must not welcome them. We must not trust them. We must cast them out."

There seemed to be an attentive agreement among the people listening. "This is a test. We are being tested by God to see if we shall worship these living statues. They have brought us a message that this is the end, but if we listen to them, this will be the end."

Molly considered his message. She had been brought up knowing several religions, and this was just one point of view but she wished that everyone hadn't rushed in so quickly in accepting the statues. At least until they were sure it was safe.

"For ours is a jealous God, and he will punish the children for their parents' sins."

The man looked in Molly's direction. As the only young person in the crowd, she could see where this was going. She turned on the spot and walked quickly away.

"Do not walk away from your God," shouted the man.

Molly didn't look back. She strode out alongside the lake until well away, then stopped to look out over the water and the park beyond. She was excited by the intrigue of the meeting with the statue of Sherlock Holmes, his secrecy, and perhaps the chance to find out what was really going on. She was also concerned that it was a trap. She watched the ducks and other birds on and around the lake; surely if the world was about to end, they would have sensed it.

An hour later, after much deliberation, Molly was on Westminster Bridge. She was approaching the middle of the bridge when she spotted a statue, not far from the Lion. It wasn't Sherlock Holmes. She wasn't sure who it was but she felt it was searching for her. Some people had stopped on the bridge to stare at the statue and some were talking to it, but the statue was looking over their heads, searching. She felt an urgent need to get off the bridge. There was no sign of Holmes. Was it a trap?

Molly turned to go, and walked headlong into someone. It was Gee-Gee.

"Hey," he said, acting as though she had nearly knocked him over. "What happened to you? Where did you get to?" he said.

"Quick, who is that statue?" Molly turned back and pointed.

"What statue?" said Gee-Gee looking down the length of the bridge. There was nothing but people and cars.

"Never mind," said Molly turning back. "Where did you go? I saw you talking to Emmeline Pankhurst, then the Burghers of Calais started to push me around and when I looked over, you'd gone."

"So that's what all that moaning and groaning was about. I lost sight of you and thought you'd wandered off," said Gee-Gee. "What are you doing here?"

Molly told him about going to New Scotland Yard and reporting their afternoon's experiences to the police, and meeting the statue of Sherlock Holmes.

Gee-Gee looked concerned. "I'm not sure you should have done that, Molly. Did you say anything about—"

"What you were saying in the taxi? No, mainly because I don't understand what you were going on about. As for the rest of it, they didn't believe me anyway. What were you talking about in the taxi? You seemed really worried. Tell me about the Agalmata."

"Not here Molly, and not now," said Gee-Gee.

"Were you a part of the Agalmata?" said Molly, refusing to give up.

Gee-Gee sighed. "Yes, I was but it's not what you think. It was just a group of people concerned about the future. There's nothing sinister."

"Then how come you lost your job over it, and why did you sound so serious in the taxi?"

"Look, I had some problems because I was too outspoken. I'm not like that anymore." He was looking more and more uncomfortable. "I will tell you about it, but right now I think you should go home, contact your parents and stay there until this whole thing is over."

Molly could smell something on Gee-Gee's breath, and guessed he'd been drinking. She changed the subject. "Sherlock Holmes said I would have made a good Baker Street Irregular. Who are they?"

"The Baker Street Irregulars? They were a group of street urchins who helped Sherlock Holmes find clues and solve crimes. However, it was also the name given to a special operations group during the War that was based in Baker Street. They were tasked by Churchill to snoop about and find out what was going on in London."

Molly preferred that description to street urchin. "What time is it now?" she asked.

"It's five thirty-five," said Gee-Gee.

It looked like Sherlock Holmes was not going to appear.

"He said he didn't have much time," said Molly. "I sensed he wanted to tell me something, but he didn't want the other statues to know. Maybe he's in trouble."

"I can't think why he should be," said Gee-Gee.

"This could be one of those occasions, you know, when something has gone wrong with the statues' plan. I got the impression he was trying to help, and he said he wanted to show me something about the Lion. What do you know about it?"

"The South Bank Lion? Twelve feet high, thirteen feet long and weighs thirteen tons," said Gee-Gee. "We wouldn't want that coming alive. It was designed by W.F. Woodington, but it is made of Coade stone."

"What's Coade stone?"

"It's not real. Discovered by Eleanor Coade, it's a really hard artificial stone."

"Code as in secret code?"

"It's spelt differently. C O A D E. Do you think that's what he was trying to tell you?"

"Could be. What else do you know about it?"

"There were two lions made for the Lion Brewery on the South Bank. It's where the Royal Festival Hall is now. When it closed, one lion went to the rugby ground at Twickenham, the other came here to Westminster Bridge. They were preserved on the wishes of another King George, this time the Sixth. Do you think there's a connection?"

It didn't make much sense. "Who was Eleanor Coade?" said Molly.

"Hmm, now that I think about it, she called her company Lithodipyra Manufactory, and if I remember rightly, it's three Greek words meaning, stone—twice—fire."

"Wow! That must be something," said Molly.

"Must be what?" said Gee-Gee.

"Stone, as in statue," said Molly.

"They're not all made of stone," said Gee-Gee.

"Fire as in shoot?" said Molly.

"There's a firing process in making statues," said Gee-Gee.

"We should tell the police."

"I don't think we should do anything of the sorts, young lady. I think we should wait until we actually know what we are talking about. After all, if the statues have come here for genuine reasons, we will look pretty stupid."

Molly stared at him. "What, after everything that's happened today?"

"Trust me, I think we should start again tomorrow, that's the best plan."

All of a sudden, Molly felt worn out. Her feet ached and she remembered that she hadn't eaten all day.

"I think it's a good idea to get some rest," said Gee-Gee. "You've had a busy day."

Unable to think of anything else to do, or any more questions to ask, Molly conceded. She thanked him for his help and headed for the Underground. It was only after they had parted company, she remembered that she wanted to ask how he had found her on Westminster Bridge.

From the Prime Minister's point of view, the day had gone well. Myddelton, Faraday and Jenner had been given all the resources they needed to carry out their own research. They also had working with them, a number of specialists in the fields of conservation, meteorology, glaciology and oceanography.

A group of distinguished historians, together with a group of distinguished statues, were in the process of rewriting history, as told by the people who were there at the time. History books had served us well up to now, often the views or impressions of the author; here was an opportunity to hear it first-hand.

Another group had been set up to handle all the external calls and enquiries. At first, much of the world had seen this as an elaborate hoax, an illusion. Now, representatives from many countries were arriving in London to see for themselves. The phenomenon of statues coming to life, was exclusive to London, although a watchful eye was being kept on statues elsewhere. The Prime Minister was enjoying taking calls from all the major powers; it asserted his position in all of this.

A mixed team of scientists had been commissioned to study how stone and metal could come to life. The statue of Thomas Guy had come forward to assist. A charitable man in the seventeen hundreds, he had been a bookseller dealing mainly in Bibles, a governor of St Thomas' and the founder of Guy's hospitals.

So far, the scientists had two schools of thought. There were those who were relying on basic physics; Einstein's $E = mc^2$, where energy and mass are different forms of the same thing. The mass, being the statue, had found a way of releasing the stored energy. There were others who were viewing it as purely spiritual; our living souls, unlike our bodies, had been preserved until they could exercise themselves again in the form of sculptures and statues. There was much debate.

Experiments were being carried out to investigate how the statues moved, and how the solid structure was becoming pliable and controllable. The potential in gaining this knowledge was enormous.

The Prime Minister was in COBR listening to the chief scientist on the latest developments.

"Tests so far," said the scientist, who had already been briefed by the Prime Minister's aide, to keep it simple. "All the usual ones: temperature, blood pressure, breathing rate, responses and ECG. Some samples were taken, we checked first that it wouldn't hurt. These were examined under an electron microscope. We've x-rayed and used ultrasound. CT scans have produced a layer-by-layer image of the inside of the statue. We then used a Cyra laser, which is a machine used for detecting hairline fractures in aircraft wings. It was used some years ago on the statue of Liberty and much of the architecture of Michelangelo. We did this on the arm of the statue in one position, and then again after it had moved. We've been trying to identify any molecular changes."

The Prime Minister nodded in understanding. This all sounded good. "What have you come up with?" he asked.

"All of these tests have consistently revealed one thing," said the scientist.

"Excellent" said the Prime Minister. "What is it?"

"The statue is made of brass," said the scientist.

The Prime Minister's next briefing was with some of his Ministers. There was an overview of the traffic situation. There appeared to be as many people trying to leave London, presumably in fear of the statues, as there were trying to enter London to see them. The police were doing a good job, using certain routes for evacuation and others for the control of those coming into the city.

Unfortunately, the Press had started to focus on the apprehension and mistrust some people were feeling. Terror, was a word being used a great deal. There was footage of the elderly leaving their homes, and of hospitals trying to relocate patients who had expressed the wish to leave the capital.

"I just don't know," said the Prime Minister. "You appear on television as the leader of the country with the sole intension of reassuring everyone, then there's always someone who has to stir it all up."

Staff tutted and sighed in agreement, and in sympathy with their leader's efforts. Another Minister reported that the last twenty-four hours had seen a mass increase in people attending religious services throughout the country. Churches were being packed out in some areas. Clearly, the overtones of living statues proving that there is life after death, was going to have an enormous impact on science and faith, and that some, who were previously non-believers, were not going to leave it to chance.

"We've cases of people trying to construct sculptures of deceased family members and loved ones, in an attempt to bring them back," said the Secretary of State for Health. "This has the potential to get seriously out of hand. The value of life could easily be undermined."

The statue of Winston Churchill had drifted into the room during the Secretary's comments.

"It's to be expected," said the statue.

The Prime Minister looked at Churchill. "Will it work?" he said.

"Only certain statues will come to life, Prime Minister. We have come to give you a message and to help you to act. It serves no purpose to have every man and his dog."

"So who decides?"

"I do," said Churchill. "Why, do you have someone in mind you would like to bring back?"

"No, no, just trying to understand how it all works."

"And you want to know if there is a higher being? Someone in overall command? Is there God?"

Everyone in the room was silent.

Churchill nodded. "A natural question. It's also natural that people will be fearful, there's only so much they can comprehend."

"But you're no threat to us?" the PM questioned.

"You know how these things work, Prime Minister. The public's range of intelligence, education and common sense is huge, and we have to accommodate everyone's understanding. Something I learned over the years.

The briefing continued with plans that had been drawn up for the next few days and following weeks. London was now the focus of the world's attention and the opportunities for Great Britain were fantastic. A little too fantastic to handle right now, but here he was, the Prime Minister, the man of the moment. It couldn't get any better.

"I'd like Robert Peel to go to New Scotland Yard, to help the police with organising things and to answer any questions they might have." Churchill was addressing the Prime Minister, and indirectly, the Commissioner.

The Commissioner shrugged. "What, as well as Sherlock Holmes?"

"Sherlock Holmes!" thundered Churchill, turning to face the Commissioner. "Sherlock Holmes! How in blazes ..."

The room fell silent.

Churchill recovered himself. "Yes, yes, of course, I remember now, Sherlock Holmes, from outside Baker Street station."

"I thought you'd sent him," said the Commissioner.

"Yes, yes, well I want Peel to replace him, better man, more suited to the job in hand. See to it will you, Commissioner. I would like him in there, immediately."

The Prime Minister was curious. That's three errors the statues have made: the Royal Marines, Alcock and Brown, and now Sherlock Holmes, so, perhaps Churchill's not completely in control.

The journey home took ages. Molly's feet hurt even more; there hadn't been a seat on the tube until Euston. She slouched as she allowed the escalator to take her to the surface and then headed home. A hot bath would see her right. Going to the Police had been a complete waste of time, and she had no idea what to make of Sherlock Holmes. Perhaps Charlie might have some ideas.

She swung open the garden gate with her foot, while searching her bag for the front door key. An icy shiver shot up the back of her neck, and she froze. There was someone in the garden. She hadn't seen anything, just sensed it. She stood, hesitating, with a hand still in her bag.

Move! Move Molly, move!

She turned and sprinted, straight across the road, and ducked down behind a parked car. She hadn't run far but was panting and out of breath. She peered over the bonnet to see her attacker.

Nothing; no one came out of the gate, no one cried out, no one chased. She was alone in the empty street. She felted stupid. She glanced at her watch, it was gone seven thirty. Charlie should be at home, but the house was in darkness. Why was the house in darkness? Why wasn't Charlie home? She considered knocking at a neighbours, but what would she say?

She started to slowly walk back, prepared to sprint again, and searched around in her bag for her mobile. She rang the house, and then cursed herself as her phone lit up her position. There was no reply at first, and then it was answered. It was her Mum's voice on the answer phone. She hung up and pressed in Charlie's mobile number.

"Hiya, Ratbag, you ok?" came her brother's chirpy reply.

"Where the hell are you?" demanded Molly, cupping her hand over the mouthpiece.

"I'm at Amber's. Where are you, didn't you get my note?"

"I'm at home, well I'm outside. I thought there was someone in our garden."

"What? Did you see someone?"

"No, but I sensed someone was there. It's probably just me being jumpy, there's no sign of anyone."

It started to rain.

"Are you happy to go in?" said Charlie. "I can stay on the phone."

Molly considered that a good idea. She slung her bag over a shoulder and cautiously walked towards her house with the phone pressed tight against her ear. Charlie was talking about nothing, just being a voice. She pushed open the gate and walked onto the path. Just as she got close to the house, the security light came on, lighting up the whole of the small garden. It was clear that there hadn't been anyone there otherwise the light would have come on.

Molly put the key in the lock and pushed open the front door. She waited. The house was in darkness and quiet. She stepped in. Everything looked normal, but she kept Charlie on the phone until she had put on all the lights and looked into every room and cupboard.

"There's a note on the kitchen table," said Charlie. "I'm sorry about this Moll, but Amber needed me. She's been pretty frightened about these statues."

"What about me needing you? I'm your sister whom you've known for fifteen years. You're supposed to be looking after me. What do you think Mum and Dad would say?"

"Since when have you needed looking after? You always do your own thing anyway."

"Oh, thanks a lot. Now we have a girlfriend, nothing else matters."

"And you're only saying that because I've got someone and you haven't."

Molly bit her lip and stopped herself from expressing an opinion of Amber. She picked up a piece of paper from the kitchen table. "I've got your note. What's with the red paint?"

"Eh?" said Charlie.

"Never mind. Look, I'll see you when I see you. I hope Amber is feeling happier," she added with sarcasm.

"Molly," said Charlie. "You won't tell Mum and Dad, will you?"

Molly hung up. She read the note.

Dear Miss Molly,

My profound apologies for frightening you this evening. You are a clever young lady; I wonder what gave me away. I was unable to keep our earlier engagement. I ask you to try again, Coade stone Lion 9 o'clock tomorrow morning. It is of the utmost importance. SH

PS Take care, your life may be in danger.

It was as though someone had gently blown on the back of her neck. She froze; the statue had been in her house. She grabbed her mobile, and pressed for Charlie's mobile. Then hung up. If Sherlock Holmes had wanted to harm her, he could have done so easily by waiting inside. What if he was trying to help? What if he did have some important message about this whole business? Why the Lion? Was it a code? And why was her life in danger? She was now certain of two things: the statues were up to no good, and she needed help to prove this.

Molly took a hot bath, dressed into pyjamas and prepared some cheese on toast and a mug of hot chocolate. She had searched the house twice more, and checked all windows and doors before getting into the bath, and now felt reassured. She opened her laptop, and typed in Coade stone Lion. She read that Eleanor Coade had created this hardwearing artificial stone to a secret recipe, which, until recently, had never been replicated. There were examples of Coade stone in St George's Chapel in Windsor Castle, where the screen in the nave is made from it. There is also a memorial to the death of Nelson made from Coade stone at the Royal Naval Hospital in Greenwich. Neither of these things meant anything to her.

There was some stuff on Eleanor Coade. Where she was born and lived, that she was a businesswoman and how she came about putting the company together. Molly read all of it. At the end, she was sure that she knew all she could know about Eleanor and her Coade stone. Exhausted, she climbed into bed, confident that she hadn't missed anything.

What she had missed, were the urgent messages on the answer phone. All of them from her parents.

Wednesday ...

Molly felt as though she hadn't slept for most of the night. It was just after five in the morning, and it was still dark outside. She was bothered and restless, and her legs felt as though they needed to be running. She turned on her bedside lamp, propped herself up on one elbow and looked around her room. She had resisted posters of pop idols and film stars, as with her friends, and had instead pictures of wildlife and nature scenes on her walls. There was one advertising the plight of orang-utans, and some framed photographs that she had actually taken herself.

She made an instant decision. Throwing back the bedclothes, she dressed in jeans and a top, trading the smart shoes she wore yesterday for her familiar trainers. She picked up her shoulder bag as it still had her mobile and other useful things in it, and headed for the door. Outside there was a glint of light from daybreak but the weather didn't look promising, so she grabbed her jacket as she left.

It felt daring going out at this time of the morning although she had no real idea what she was going to do. She had decided to meet Sherlock Homes at the Coade stone Lion, but that wasn't until nine. It did mean she could get there early and check it out, but what to do in the meantime?

She started walking down Fitzjohn's Avenue, in the general direction of Swiss Cottage. The morning air was cold, and autumn had certainly arrived. She thought about her brother being in Amber's house and wondered whether Amber's parents would allow Charlie and their daughter to share a bedroom. Molly really liked her brother. It would have been good to have him with her now. She'd always believed they'd made a good team, although recently she'd noticed Charlie getting interested in other things. The television, trashy celebrity shows, and electronic gadgets seemed to feature more now. He used to enjoy messing about with mechanical things and getting broken things to work.

She walked into Avenue Road where she admired many of the expensive looking cars parked behind electronic gates. This led her to Regent's Park, which would make for a pleasant walk, so she joined the Outer Circle, the path that runs around the park, and headed for the lake. From there, she walked onto Baker Street.

Baker Street, of course, the home of Sherlock Holmes, he might be on his plinth outside the railway station. Where else do statues go at nighttime? She might be able to speak to him right now.

She scooted round the corner into Marylebone Road and found him. Standing at the base of his statue, she looked up into his face. He was motionless. She tapped her knuckles on one of his legs. It made a sound, exactly as it should have done.

"Mr Holmes," she said, looking up at him again. "It's me, Molly Hargreaves." She felt silly doing this but it had to be done. An expressionless face was her only greeting.

"Please speak to me. I need your help. I need to ask you about the ..." she whispered the word, "...Agalmata."

She spoke to him several times but there was no response. Why wasn't he answering? What did this mean?

"I got your note," she said hoping to promote some response. "Are we still on for nine o'clock?"

There was nothing. Molly quickly came to the conclusion that wasn't that Sherlock Holmes was choosing to be silent, it was that he had been silenced.

She knew exactly what she had to do next.

Molly got to Parliament Square and Westminster Bridge as soon as she could. Normally, at this early hour, there would be the odd cyclist, some street cleaners, an early jogger, and the streets would be quiet; the statues had changed all that, and there were quite a few people about. The area directly around the Houses of Parliament had been cordoned off and was being guarded by police.

Molly walked onto the bridge, taking the opposite side of the road to the statue of Boudicca. If the Queen of Iceni was going to move, Molly wanted as much warning as possible. She crossed over the bridge, passed the Lion and then doubled back, having checked that no one was following her. The Lion, looked stark white, majestic on its huge granite blocks.

What was it that Sherlock Holmes wanted to tell her about the Coade stone Lion? 'Something of the utmost importance,' he'd said. Was he going to tell her or show her? Both meeting places had been here, so assuming that it wasn't just a convenient meeting place, and there was that possibility, he must have wanted to show her something.

Molly wondered if it might be something on the Lion itself. She had read on the internet that when the Lion had been moved, a time capsule from had been found. It had contained a business card for the Coade factory and two William IV coins. Was there a connection?

She tried to climb the granite to get a closer look at the Lion, but it wasn't easy as the stone was polished. There was a signpost right next to one corner of the monument with fingerboards pointing to the Houses of Parliament and Westminster Abbey. She pictured being able to use the post as a way of getting onto the Lion's plinth and then, maybe finding a clue. The signpost wobbled as she clung to it and the thin metal boards were sharp and dug into her hand, and she didn't have the strength to pull herself up. She jumped back down, fell awkwardly and landed on her bottom. Some Baker Street Irregular you would have made, she said to herself.

Molly sat down on the step, and thought about Sherlock Holmes. He said he didn't have much time, that implied he was in danger. He had something of the utmost importance to tell or show her, and for that to have been really important and needing secrecy, it had to be something about the statues that wasn't to their benefit. If he believed he wasn't going to be able to meet with her, presuming he had been turned back to a statue to stop him saying anything, he might try to leave the information somewhere. A written note may have been difficult for him to write and where would he leave it to be sure someone else didn't get it instead? Could he have passed the information on? There was no one else about. If it had been to another statue, he would have needed to trust them and that seemed unlikely.

Molly looked around, picturing Holmes having to quickly think on his feet. He knew she would come here. He knew the other statues were on to him. He would have had to improvise something.

Part of the bridge had scaffolding and boarding on it and she read a sign, across the road that told her about the bridge developments for the next two years. On one end of the parapet was a paint pot with a paint-brush sticking out of it. Now that she had noticed it, it looked out of place. It was too early for any workmen. Perhaps one of them had left it out, but it just didn't look right.

Molly walked across the road and looked at the pot. It was red paint and the bridge was light green in colour. Red paint! The note from Sherlock Holmes. She had left it home but remembered that it had finger marks on it in red paint. One on the written side and two on the other, as if the writer had picked it up to read it with paint on his hands. It was more than just a note.

She looked over the parapet. The scaffolding continued right underneath and to the other side. There were some thick black cables secured to the bridge with plastic ties, and a yellow triangular sticker next to them saying, *Danger 414 Volts*, but definitely no red paint.

Molly felt certain that Holmes had been here, she could feel it. If she wanted to know for sure, if she wanted to prove what the statues were up to, if she wanted to find any message from Holmes; she'd have to be brave.

She gave a good look around to make sure no one was watching, and then pulled herself up onto the parapet. Swinging her legs over, she was now directly above the water but with the scaffolding below her. A cool breeze passed across her face giving her an impression of exposure. She just needed to lower herself onto the scaffolding and then she would have access to the underside of the bridge.

Swivelling onto her tummy and edging herself to the edge, she found a handhold in an ornate piece of stonework, made up of three circles all linked together. She wriggled three fingers of both hands into two hand-holds in order to get the best grip. The stone was angled and dusty and not the easiest thing to hold on to.

It looked an awfully long way down and the river menacing with its dark water being lapped up by the current and wind. If she fell, she would hit the scaffolding, then probably slip through, straight down to the river and drown. Molly also remembered that most bridge stanchions got wider just below the surface so she risked hitting that as well.

This wasn't getting her anywhere. There was nothing else for it, she just had to go for it. Committing all her weight to the ornate stone, Molly lowered herself onto her arms, her toes searched for the scaffolding.

Where the hell is it?

In an instant, Molly lost her nerve and panic set in. She tried to reverse her descent by pulling on her arms but fear had made her weak and her arms refused to cooperate. She thought about crying out for help but couldn't quite manage the conviction to do so, and now she was hyper-ventilating.

Her hand, injured on the signpost, was stinging with pain and she was beginning to lose her grip. Her eyes searched for something to grab onto. She looked at the bundled, black, electric cables and grabbed them with one hand.

Please don't let me be electrocuted.

The plastic cable-ties securing the cable to the bridge stretched but didn't break, and neither was she electrocuted. She used the cables to lower herself onto the scaffolding, then onto the wooden planking that lay across the scaffolding.

"What are you doing, girl?" Molly said aloud, her voice echoing under the bridge. The panic over, she grinned, partly from an involuntary reflex from being scared, but also because she was having an adventure.

She had no idea how she was going to get back up.

Molly shuffled slowly forward feeling her way as underneath the bridge was dark, and she was waiting for her eyes to adjust. The bridge was massive, gigantic steel girders held together by thousands of large rivets. She spotted dabs of red paint on the metalwork of the bridge, which she followed, then she reached a red line running across the wood-en planks. Molly took it to be a stop-line, and she looked around the bridge, searching every inch of structure.

Suddenly it was there. On a wide girder above her — red paint, in big words.

THE HEARTED PIRATE. SH.

Molly felt dizzy with excitement. SH – Sherlock Holmes, of course, he had been here. Molly had worked it out, she was right. Forced to leave her a clue, he had come here, and written this in big red letters, it couldn't be clearer. What did it mean? She had no idea. She took a photo with her phone, and gave a careful look on all the other girders to see if there was anything else, but they were all message-free.

Now being closer to the far side of the bridge, and believing that she was never going to make it back up, Molly shuffled on, completing the full width of the bridge. She emerged into daylight, more scaffolding and wooden planking, and, thankfully, a ladder. It ran all the way to the top of the bridge and was clearly the way the workmen accessed the underside of the bridge, and probably the way Sherlock Holmes had come.

Feeling stupid that she hadn't spotted it before but pleased with herself for what she had done, she scrambled up the metal rungs. She was safe and she'd found the clue. The Hearted Pirate, she'd never heard of that but she could ask Gee-Gee and Charlie and there was always the internet.

The ladder took her to some short scaffolding poles, which aided her getting back over the stone parapet. She hadn't been able to see the ladder as all this side was hidden by high wooden boarding. There was a door to the pavement, and of course, it could be opened from her side. With feelings of relief, and success, she stepped out onto the street.

A cold, stone hand grabbed hold of her wrist. The hand squeezed and Molly yelped.

From nine feet above her, the statue of Edith Cavell looked stern and impatient as though she had caught a naughty girl doing something wrong. Molly tried to pull away but it was hopeless. The stone hand grazed her wrist, and she looked for someone who might help, but here was no one.

Dwarfed by the statue, Molly felt sick as her stomach churned. She so regretted not checking before stepping out onto the pavement.

"Come with me," the statue commanded, pulling Molly behind her and heading towards the Coade stone Lion. Molly's shoes scuffed as she tried to resist being pulled, but the statue had immense strength. They didn't stop at the Lion but turned left, down the steps to the river. A river barge was moored against the side with a plank of wood resting from the bank to the lip of the barge's hold.

Cavell shoved Molly forward across the wooden plank, and for the second time that morning, she risked falling into the Thames. She stepped onto the metal barge as Edith Cavell stepped across the gap without using the plank. The statue took hold of Molly's wrists and lowered her, with ease, into the open hold. Molly looked up; all she could see now was the bridge and the top half of the London Eye, that and the grey sky above. The barge was empty, the steel walls were rusty, and there was smell of damp earth.

"Where are you taking me?" Molly said, trying to be brave. "It's the Tower for you. That will teach you not to interfere."

The statue cast off, and the barge pitched a little as it joined the main flow. Molly staggered sideways, losing her balance. Her footsteps made a hollow echo inside the metallic hold. She propped an arm against one side in order to steady herself, still watching the statue.

Cavell's movements were slow but deliberate, just like the other statues. She differed in her colour, the stone looked off-white with a grey speck and in places, had been stained from berry-eating birds. There was no cracking of stone as the statue moved, no expression on her face and no signs of any emotion. It seemed perfectly balanced in the barge and was still able to see out when stood in the hold. It occurred to Molly that Cavell must have known that she would be here, the barge being ready and waiting. She wondered how. Her mind raced through all the facts she could remember about Cavell and how that might help her. She had been a nurse working for the Red Cross; she was from Norfolk and her father had been a vicar; she liked ice skating, flowers and was an accomplished artist and as a girl, she had used this skill to raise money for a church room for Sunday school. Molly didn't think that any of that was going to help.

They passed under three bridges, one after another and it occurred to Molly that she should take note of where she was going. The next bridge was all-concrete. The barge made a steady turn to the right.

She recognised Blackfriars, then the Millennium footbridge and as they passed underneath there was a dreadful thump-thump noise as a jogger passed overhead. The bridge didn't sound particularly solid. There was the City of London School, and the Tate Modern on the other side with the Globe Theatre next to it. Southwark Bridge, plain old London Bridge; Molly caught a glimpse of the big fish on the top of Billingsgate Market, which she'd never noticed before.

They had been travelling for about thirty minutes, when the barge lost power and drifted to the left. From inside the hold, Molly could see the familiar features of Tower Bridge as they came under one of the abutment towers that help to hold the two main towers in place.

The barge came to a stop. The statue climbed out and reached down for

Molly, lifting her by her two wrists, as before. She lowered her down onto a cobblestoned ramp that climbed from the river, to a series of concrete steps and an archway. The archway was lined with white tiles, the sort you get in underground stations.

This was not a nice place. There was a pungent smell of all things bad. The river water looked dank and dirty with lots of debris floating on the surface. The ramp was brown and slimy from being repeatedly under water, and to the right was a wooden pier; a rook glided passed and settled on one of its thick beams.

To the left was a small shingle beach. There were some old damaged drainpipes sticking out of the ground, a worn car tyre and pieces of wood, probably from a packing case.

And a man.

There was a man combing the beach with a metal detector. He had on, a blue woollen hat, overalls and wellington boots and headphones over his ears.

Would he hear her if she screamed? Molly screamed. She screamed with all her might.

"Help!"

A stone hand grabbed her by the throat but Molly twisted out of it before it tightened. She powered her legs across the ramp and onto the beach. The shingle gave way with every stride but she pumped her arms and ran as she'd never run before.

The man was still looking at the ground although his head was slightly raised. Molly was sure he must be able to see her, she was running straight at him. She cried out again but the exertion stifled her words. She didn't look back at the statue; she knew she would hear the crunching noise of the statue reaching the shingle. She got to the man and dug her feet in to stop, so as not to knock him over.

"Please, help me," she said.

The man put the metal detector into his left hand and grabbed her wrist with his right, the same wrist Cavell had injured when it had captured her. Molly was shocked at the man's actions. He held her wrist up in the air as if she was the winner of a boxing match, and looked towards the statue as it took long casual strides towards her.

"What are doing?" said Molly. She tried to pull away from the man but he was too strong. The statue was almost to them. Molly kicked out at the man's shins. He cried out and dropped his metal detector but hung on to Molly's wrist.

Cavell got there, Molly cowered. The statue reached down, put a powerful arm around Molly's chest, and lifted her clean off the ground into a vertical position. Molly was in a stone vice. The statue strode back across the beach and up the cobblestone ramp carrying Molly with ease. She caught a glimpse of the man again, now rubbing his shin. Why hadn't he helped her? Why was he helping the statue?

It was becoming harder and harder to breathe, as the statue gripped tighter and tighter. They had reached the top of the ramp, turned left and were now climbing a series of algae stained, concrete steps. Molly tried to protest but could no longer get the words out. At the top of the steps, they turned into the archway.

Molly started to panic. She couldn't inflate her chest, her head was swimming and she had pinpricks of light in front of her eyes. She tried beating the arm of the statue with her fists, but she was punching stone.

I am going to die and I don't think it's on purpose; the statue hasn't realised that I cannot breathe.

She could just make out some blue railings as they approached an old wooden door that didn't have a handle. The statue touched the door, it opened, and Molly was carried inside. At that point, everything went black.

Charlie was feeling guilty. He had caught an early train from Swiss Cottage to Hampstead Heath, and jogged all the way to the house. He quietly let himself in, not wanting to wake Molly but hoped she was actually up so he could speak to her. He shouldn't have left her all night, and knew that he had betrayed the trust of his parents. They didn't have to know of course, but he was regretting his words to her on the phone, and he needed to make sure that his sister was all right.

The house was still. Charlie quietly tiptoed up the stairs. Molly's bedroom door was open and the bed looked as though it had been slept in, but no Molly. He called out. He checked the bathroom, their parents' bedroom and then rang her mobile. There was no reply. The answer phone was showing five messages. Charlie pressed the button and heard his father's voice.

"Molly, Charlie, call us, as soon as you get this. I want you both to stay indoors. We've heard what's going on and you are in danger. We're trying to get a flight home ..."

Mum's voice in the background interrupted Dad's. "Why aren't they answering their phones?"

"—call us son, stay in, it's not safe, we're coming home."

Charlie could easily detect the stress in his father's voice. The second message was loading as Charlie found the note from Sherlock Holmes. He tore out of the house and headed back to the tube station.

Molly woke feeling cold. Her breathing was painful and her chest bruised. She'd never passed out before but guessed she hadn't been out for long. She sat up, slowly. The room she was in was oblong-shaped with more of those old white tiles on the walls. It looked clinical but old and dirty. There was a musty smell and the light was poor. There were two doors; the first, she guessed, was the one she had been brought in through; the other looked like it went deeper into the building.

Molly was sitting on one of three identical tables of white stone, which could have been marble. She pulled her knees up to her chest and wrapped her arms around them to keep warm. There was no sign of the statue.

She tried her hardest not to cry. Her thoughts turned to Mum and Dad, and then her brother; she pictured her bedroom and one or two of her friends. She wished more than anything to be free again. The tears started to roll down her cheeks. They tickled a little and she wiped them with the fleshy part of the base of her thumb. It fitted perfectly into her eye socket, as if made for the job of wiping away tears.

Statues don't cry. Molly disliked them even more now. Why do we build them, and why do we build them so big? She had read about Charles I, who at only five feet four tall, wished he was taller and ordered that his statue be made to six feet; such vanity. This statue of Cavell was easily nine feet tall. Why did we make such idols of dead people, did we think we would forget them without something in stone?

You had only to look into history to see that the so-called statue-worthy people were not always good, nor were they always responsible for the things we remember them for. Sometimes the achievement or sacrifice had been made by someone else. All this stuff about conservation and people listening to them as if they were — well, Gods.

Molly was beginning to feel better already. The mental talk she had given herself about the worthlessness of statues was working. She had met some worthy people from her travels with Mum and Dad, none of whom would be honoured with a statue of themselves.

She looked around; her bag with mobile phone and purse were gone, presumably taken by the statue. She jumped down off the marble table and walked over to an old central heating boiler that was covered in dust. If the building had heating that might mean people. Alongside the boiler were several cardboard boxes, stacked on top of each other. She opened one to find old leaflets for the Tower Bridge Exhibition. Clearly, the room was being used as a storeroom. She was putting the leaflets back just as something brown and fast scurried away across the floor and under the boiler. Mice, or even worse, rats.

Charlie reached the Lion with a sense of dread, and he concentrated on subduing this emotion. The journey had taken ages as it was the start of the rush hour, made worse by all the road closures and other police controls. He searched around the Coade stone Lion but there was no sign of his sister. He peered over the embankment wall and looked at the river, the colour and murkiness gave it an all-concealing look. It didn't bear thinking about. In desperation, he started asking people walking by.

"Excuse me, have you seen a young girl hanging around here this morning?"

"Can you help please, I've lost my young sister? She's about this tall?"

"Excuse me, have you seen a fifteen year old girl, with fair hair, she might have been here earlier?"

There was nothing positive. Most people were on their way to work and just passing through.

Charlie walked down the steps towards the river. There was a man asleep on a concrete bench. The man had long, unkempt, grey hair and a beard to match. He also had a strong unwashed smell that Charlie easily detected. Charlie guessed the man to be homeless and that he probably slept here every night. Charlie gently shook the man's shoulder. There was no response. He tried again more firmly. "Excuse me," he said, not sure whether to call him mate or sir.

There was still no response.

The man was curled up in an old, torn anorak with the hood up. Next to him and within his reach, were three plastic carrier bags that were perhaps his worldly possessions. Charlie curiously peered into one of the carrier bags.

The man woke instantly and sat up. "What's your game?" he said.

"I'm really sorry to wake you, sir," said Charlie. "My sister has gone missing. I think she was here this morning and now I can't find her. She's only fifteen, about five feet tall, probably with a brightly coloured shoulder bag."

"She was with a statue," said the man without any other prompting.

"What?" said Charlie.

"Didn't look good. The statue was dragging her down there." The man pointed towards the river. "I heard the statue say that she was taking her to the Tower of London."

Charlie was panic-stricken — Molly, taken by a statue. This was the worst possible outcome. "How long ago?" said Charlie.

"Dunno," said the tramp, "I ain't got no watch."

Charlie wanted to blame the man for his sister's disappearance, or at least for not having done something about it. Instead, he turned to the steps that led to the parapet and looked down to the water. Perhaps they had gone off in a boat.

Charlie needed the Police and knew there would be plenty in Parliament Square. He ran back up the steps, leaving the man who was already asleep again. He turned right onto the bridge, sprinted back to the Houses of Parliament, and ran to the first policeman he saw.

The sprint over the bridge left Charlie breathless. He felt flushed, and the sweat from his forehead was mixing with the watering of his eyes. He blinked several times to stop the stinging

"You've got to come with me. I need your help," he said to the first police officer he saw. In his rush to get the words out, Charlie's spittle landed on the officer's uniform. The officer wiped it and then held his hand out as if to show Charlie the evidence.

"Why don't you just slow down, son," said the officer as he reached into a trouser pocket for a handkerchief, "and tell me what's going on."

Charlie took a lungful of air. "My name is Charlie Hargreaves, and I live in Hampstead Heath. I am seventeen years old. My sister, Molly, has been taken by a statue. She went missing this morning and I just spoke with that man over there," he pointed in the direction of the far side of the bridge, "and he told me she was dragged to the river by a statue."

"Are you serious?" said the officer.

"Absolutely," said Charlie.

The officer waved at a colleague to indicate he was leaving his post to go with Charlie, and the two of them marched over the bridge. Charlie told the officer everything he considered relevant about Molly, and what had happened so far.

They found the man still asleep in the same position. He protested at being woken a second time, even if it was by an officer of the law, but gave an account of what he had seen. The officer then spoke at length on his radio, walking back up onto Westminster Bridge as he did so.

"We're going to search the Tower," said the officer when he'd finished speaking. "I want you to go there so you can give my colleagues a description and anything else they need. I've called for a car to take you."

Charlie could already hear a siren approaching, and by the time he had thanked the officer, a police car was pulling up alongside them, it's, blue lights and headlights flashing.

Molly heard footsteps. She shot back to where she had being lying and made out she was still unconscious, then changed her mind and sat upright just as the door opened. The statue stooped and entered the room. Molly glared and did her best to look confident.

"You're awake then," said the statue. "You shouldn't have run off."

"Why have you brought me here? Said Molly.

The statue didn't answer.

"Who was that man? Why didn't he help me?"

Still no answer.

"Why are you doing this?"

"Because we must," said the statue.

"Why must you?"

Again, no reply.

Molly tried a different tack. "I need to pee," she said.

The statue shrugged. "Go in the corner."

"When you were alive you were a nurse, a good person," said Molly. "You helped soldiers escape from occupied Belgium and into Holland."

"And they executed me for it."

Molly couldn't think of what to say next.

"Did you know that the British government chose not to help?" continued the statue. "The American's made representation but it didn't do any good."

"I know it must have been horrible for you, but why have you taken me?"

"Because you are meddling in things you don't understand."

"Then explain them to me," said Molly. "I'm willing to learn."

The statue paused for a moment. "When I was a nurse, I strove hard to help, I believed in what was right and what was wrong. Even when I was executed, I stood by my convictions and was proud of what I had achieved."

Molly listened.

"We have seen the steady deterioration of a system that creates and maintains life. Mankind has polluted the air, sterilised the land and infected the water. In time, nothing will survive. You claim to be doing something about it, but you are so easily distracted by other things."

"So you've come here to help us?"

"If you like."

"What does that mean?"

"Like you, we want to survive. We shall survive."

"Who is, we, exactly?"

"We are the spirits of our former selves. You created a presence for us here, when you made figures of us."

"So you've come back from the dead?"

"Not exactly, we are different now, better. We have collective thought and experiences, and with all the centuries of knowledge, learning, understanding, we can achieve more."

The statue looked determined.

"Consider this," the statue continued. "You are soft flesh that needs to be sustained with food and water. You get sick. You suffer with weak, human qualities. You have not learnt by your mistakes. History is merely an interest to you."

Molly wanted to tell the statue that she found history important, but now was not the time to interrupt.

"We are none of those things," said the statue." We have evolved and we can add to our numbers simply by building more statues. You say I was a good person, well, I. am doing this now for the greater good. You will destroy yourselves and everything around you. We cannot allow that. I am not the Edith Cavell I was, I am something new. We are the new species."

Molly stared in absolute disbelief. This was scary stuff. She took a gamble. "What's the Agalmata got to do with all this?" she said.

"What do you know of the Agalmata?" said the statue turning its head slightly to one side. The statue smiled. "Yes, of course. We enjoy their support and assistance. How do you think I knew where you would be this morning? You asked who was the man on the beach and why didn't he help you escape? The Agalmata have existed for a very long time, and like us, they care about the future of this world."

"But they're a secret?" said Molly. "They exist in secrecy. Secret societies are seldom good."

"You would be surprised who are members," said the statue.

"I know someone," said Molly.

"You're referring to Geoffrey Gray."

"So, he *is* a member of the Agalmata!"

"And so is your father," said the statue.

The words were crushingly spoken. Molly was stunned. She tried to think of a response. No way — I don't believe you — you're just saying that, but none of that seemed appropriate. She didn't believe it, but why would the statue say such a thing?

"Not so sure of ourselves now, are we Molly," said the statue. "You'll have to ask your father yourself but listen to this. He once suggested that you would make a good member.

It was a betrayal of everything she knew and understood. Her father, maybe her mother as well, members of a secret society that were in league with living statues. That they had kept this from her and had exposed her, to what — she had no idea. She started to question the timing of her parents' expedition to Peru.

"You've had a couple of recent encounters with statues," said the statue. "Forster and Eisenhower; they've known things about you. We all know about you. You could say, you have been of special interest to us, Molly Hargreaves."

Molly couldn't speak. Surely, her own father hadn't been telling the statues about her life. For what purpose?

"Soon, you will appreciate that all this is for your own good," said the statue.

Somehow, there was something in what the statue was saying, as though there was a distant memory locked away in Molly's head.

"Come with me," Cavell ordered.

Molly was powerless to refuse. She followed through the second doorway, which led to a circular, stone staircase. As Molly climbed the stairs, she noted how difficult it was for the statue, being too large for the restrictive opening. At times, the statue had both hands and feet on the stone steps. Molly wondered where the staircase led to and whether this was an opportunity to escape. She could easily outpace the statue, but if it led nowhere she'd just make matters worse.

Now and again, there was a small lead latticed window and Molly tried to get a glimpse through each one as she walked up. The statue told her to stop alongside one of them.

"Take a look," said the statue.

Molly peered through the glass. It was grey and dirty but she had a reasonable view of the Tower of London, which was being searched by lots of police officers, on foot, with dogs and even a couple on horseback. There were two police cars and an ambulance parked on the bridge road.

"They are looking for you," said the statue, "but in the wrong place, of course."

The police car tore off with sirens wailing. Charlie sat in the back, rolling with the corners being taken at speed. He fumbled for his seat belt, searching for one end, then decided not to bother, the whole journey would be over by the time he'd found it.

The police car joined Victoria Embankment, weaving in between other cars and keep-left bollards, and passing through three sets of traffic lights, all on red. The sirens echoed off the surrounding buildings, and the driver took the engine to maximum revs before each gear change; the acceleration was exhilarating. No wonder people became police officers.

At one stage, they were on the wrong side of the road for the entire length of the cars ahead of them. A moped rider pulled out between two queuing vehicles. The police driver hit the brakes and swerved, and it was all very controlled.

"What else do we need on this thing to tell them we're coming?" the driver said to his colleague.

They reached the road that goes over Tower Bridge, where they did a three-point turn and stopped behind two police cars and an ambulance. The colleague used the radio, giving a code to say that they had arrived.

"We'll take you to our command post," said the colleague. Charlie stepped out of the vehicle, a little giddy from the whole experience. He looked across at the Tower of London. This great fortress with centuries of history had once more become a prison. This time for his sister.

Molly could hear more sirens and she turned back to her window. She rubbed it with her fingers, but it refused to be any cleaner. There was another police car arriving, its headlights were flashing. The car did a three-point turn and stopped behind the other two. She pressed her face to the window, willing whoever got out of the vehicle to look up and see her.

The doors of the police car opened and out stepped — her brother. Oh my God, it was Charlie. Molly furiously banged on the window, which seemed to be made of toughened glass and produced nothing more than a dull sound. She shouted, not caring if the statue intervened or not. She watched as Charlie stood for a moment looking towards the Tower of London and then walked off with two officers. He hadn't heard her.

Charlie was led down from the Bridge to a gravelled path that ran alongside the river and the Tower. There was a police officer there with a clipboard and someone else giving instructions to officers with dogs. Some of the police were carrying guns. There was also a group of Beefeaters in their smart red uniforms, and Charlie guessed that they were also being used in the search. The officer with the clipboard took a description of Molly: what she was wearing, did she have a mobile phone, where her parents were, and stuff like that. He explained to Charlie that this area was their command post and asked Charlie to remain in case they needed to ask him more questions. Charlie agreed, reassured that things were being done.

He was looking for somewhere to sit when he saw a well-built man with white hair watching him. The man was wearing a blue jacket and trousers that were in need of an iron. Charlie didn't think he could be police.

The man walked over.

"You must be Molly's brother?" he said.

"Yes, I am," said Charlie, curious as to how this man knew.

"My name is Gee-Gee. I have been helping your sister with this whole statue thing."

Charlie didn't make a connection.

"She might have mentioned me. My real name is Geoffrey Gray, I used to be a tour guide."

It fell into place.

"When did you last see her?" said Charlie. "Have you seen her this morning"?

"No, we parted yesterday evening, and she said she was going home."

Charlie explained that she had left this morning before he'd arrived home. He remembered the note from Sherlock Holmes, and took it out from his pocket.

I should have given it to the police," he said as Gee-Gee was reading it.

"I'm not sure it sheds any more light on the situation," said Gee-Gee.

Charlie looked for the man with the clipboard.

"Why don't you go up onto the bridge," suggested Gee-Gee as he looked towards Tower Bridge. "You can get a really good view of the Tower from there, and you might just spot her."

"Are you sure?" said Charlie, the bridge didn't look high enough.

"Well, I should know, I used to work as a tour guide."

"I was told to wait here in case the police want any more information from me."

"I'll wait if you like and I'll give you a shout if they want anything."

"Charlie considered Gee-Gee's offer and decided to go."

"Through that arch, up the steps and you'll come out by that gate, underneath that round tower," said Gee-Gee. "You can then look straight into the grounds of the Tower with a clear view," he said as he slipped the note from Sherlock Holmes into his own pocket.

"Thanks. Thanks a lot," said Charlie as he strode off.

Charlie did as instructed and quickly found himself up on the bridge road not far from where he had arrived in the police car. He walked up and down the road but there was no view into the grounds. Charlie wondered if he'd misunderstood the directions, and maybe there was a way of getting up higher, into the bridge towers.

There were some large metal plaques on the wall describing the building of Tower Bridge and next to those a wooden door. Charlie looked at it, considering whether to try the handle or not. As if willed to do so, the door opened. He looked around him to see if anyone else was watching and stepped forward to look inside.

"Hello," he called out. "Hello, is anyone there?" He peered into a small lobby, which was all stone and bare. He stepped in further. "Hello?"

"Hello," said a cold voice as the door slammed behind him.

Back at the command post, the officer with the clipboard was looking for Charlie. "Where's he gone?" he asked Gee-Gee. "I told him to stay here."

"He won't be far," said Gee-Gee. "Can I give him a message?"

"We're pulling out," said the officer. "We've done the best we can, as far as we are concerned the girl's not in there. Besides, we're needed elsewhere now, looks like all the statues are on the move and heading for somewhere."

"I'll let him know," said Gee-Gee.

Like many people in London, Nico was not born in Britain. He was Italian, and a short man of stocky build with a bulbous nose, and used his hands as much as his mouth, when speaking. He usually dressed in a tee-shirt, even when it was cold, and he worked a stall on Westminster Bridge selling tourist type things: badges and enamelled plates, umbrellas and Union flags, stickers and postcards of London, laughing, chattering plastic teeth and policemen's helmets. Being a foreigner himself, Nico appreciated why tourists bought these mementos. He did a good trade.

He also had a prime position, on a corner of a busy street and directly underneath a popular tourist attraction, Boudicca, the Queen of the Iceni.

With all the business of statues coming alive, people had gathered looking for any movement in this famous statue: a swish of a horse's tail, a turn of a chariot wheel, or for one of her daughters to cover a breast after all these years of exposure. Nico was very happy with the increase in trade.

A tourist had asked, "Are you not worried about her coming to life, dropping down and crushing your stall?"

"Nah," said Nico. "We've come to an agreement, in the interest of good business, of course."

It was about midday when there was a swish of a horse's tail. A nostril flared and there was a quiver in the large muscle across its chest. A tourist taking a picture, cried out as a horse's hoof thrashed the air. With an excruciating noise, the chariot started rocking, backwards and forewords, as it tried to pull away from its mountings, metal on metal. The two daughters didn't bother to cover up, but tightened their grip on the edge on the chariot. The horses reared higher, muscles bulging as they used all their might to get free. Boudicca urged them on.

Nico dropped his chattering teeth, as his customers went from idle curiosity, to gawping spectators, to fleeing victims in seconds.

So much for agreements in the interest of good business.

With a determined thrust, the two bronze horses took to the air, dragging the chariot behind them. They dropped instantly, their hoofs driving into the tarmac as if it was soft mud. Next came the chariot, crushing a metal roadside barrier then landing on the road with such force that two huge ruts appeared. It was the momentum of the heavy chariot that forced the horses forward as they frantically fought for their footing.

Boudicca cracked the reins; the horses reared in protest, almost unseating the passengers, and then pulled in unison as they had done so, many years before. With a sharp turn to the right, they headed for Parliament Square.

People screamed, cameras flashed, traffic screeched, some collided. Panic was all around. Police officers in fluorescent jackets ran forward as sirens wailed in the background.

Boudicca was back in town.

The police response was quick. There was a police car and motorbike pushing ahead of Boudicca with headlights flashing, blue lights and sirens. The drivers skilfully choosing the easiest route, sometimes on the wrong side of the road and jumping red traffic lights. On occasions, it looked as though they were being chased by Boudicca, and perhaps they were.

The chariot was creating great ruts in the road but the real damage was being caused by the two vicious looking blades protruding from the wheels, one on each side. Although not sharp, they easily knocked over bins, a newspaper stand and several keep-left bollards. Some roads signs and a traffic light were severed. People were falling over each other, in an effort to get out of the way.

Further up the road, some were slow to move. Not having seen what had just taken place, they froze in total disbelief, and then slammed back into reality by shouts and screams from others, and their own resilience to survive.

Boudicca urged her horses on just as her daughters, still gripping tightly, urged their mother on. Other police units were being despatched and roadblocks were being planned. News of the chase had reached New Scotland Yard, and there was a heated discussion on how to stop thirty tons of marauding bronze. Whatever they were going to do, they had to do it fast.

Taking the initiative, a police driver slammed his vehicle across the entrance to Whitehall. Sensibly he bailed out, scuffling across the pavement on all fours as the scythed chariot reached his car without slowing. Together, the two horses jumped the vehicle. A hoof hit the windscreen, smashing it instantly and the force rocked the car. The chariot followed. The elevation of the horses raised the central connecting bar so the first thing to make contact was the wheels of the chariot. They sliced through the door panels and roof of the car, as if it was made of soft tin. The officer would have been lucky to escape.

In no time, the chariot had cleared Whitehall and turned left at Trafalgar Square. The three occupants looked to the right for a moment, and Boudicca appeared to be trying to stop her chariot, but the horses had other plans, and they pulled and galloped into Pall Mall followed by a hard right into the lower end of Regent Street.

Police motorcyclists accelerated ahead, urging pedestrians to get out of the way, as the chariot passed through Piccadilly Circus and into Regent Street, just where the road then curves. Perhaps being out of practice, Boudicca over-did the turn and her chariot collided with the side of an open-topped tour bus. The bus passengers, immersed in the commentary from their individual headphones, shuddered with the impact. Shocked, foreign tourists looked down from the top onto a chariot from Roman times.

The lethal blades tore a hole in the bus, from front to rear, with a horrible jarring noise as the blades pulled out, and the chariot rocked up onto one wheel. Boudicca and her daughters clung on. Tearing a hole in one of London's double deckers was impressive, being thrown from your own chariot wasn't.

"What the bloody hell is going on?" demanded the Prime Minister to Sir Winston Churchill. "If this is another one of your so-called-glitches, acting on their own, then it's got to stop and it's got to stop now, before someone gets killed!" The Prime Minister had an opportunity to reassert some authority. He waited for some response.

"Let's talk," said Churchill. The statue turned on a heel and walked into Chambers. They were alone.

"This is going to be a difficult day for you, Prime Minister," said the statue.

The PM shrugged. "I've had plenty of those."

"You'll recall kindly inviting in three compatriots of mine; Myddelton, Faraday and Jenner? You won't have seen much of them as they have been doing some work for me.

The Prime Minister felt puzzled.

"Jenner was a good man. What he achieved was a miracle and saved many lives. Could you imagine the re-introduction of the smallpox virus?"

The Prime Minister felt uncomfortable.

"A more virulent strain, hemorrhagic smallpox, a type that doesn't just produce blisters and the detachment of layers of skin but causes organs to bleed. Even the eyes, which would turn dark red and eventually black. People are no longer vaccinated against smallpox, especially a new strain."

The Prime Minister felt scared. He didn't need to imagine, this was the sort of thing that was played out during their inter-governmental planning exercises. The training days usually ended with everyone praying that it never happens.

"Of course, one would need a delivery system for such a wicked disease," continued Churchill. "Myddelton has extensive knowledge of the fresh water system that comes into London. He should do, he built it. That would be an easy way to get a new strain of illness quickly distributed throughout London."

The Prime Minister felt unwell.

"But of course, the distribution of London's drinking water is strictly controlled with sophisticated computers, equipped with self-testing and monitoring and all linked to an alarm system. You would need to build an electro-magnetic device that could over-ride the control procedures and actually allow water to run freely into people's homes. Complete with anything that it might be carrying. Faraday was an expert on electro-magnetics."

The picture was becoming clear and it wasn't a pretty one.

"Do you think we have been idle since our deaths?" said Churchill. "We have been here amongst you for a very long time. We have accrued all your knowledge, developed it further and shared it with our collective thought."

The statue softened his tone.

"Prime Minister, we do not want anyone to come to harm but we have to take control. We could do this forcefully, there are thousands of us in London alone. You cannot harm us. You cannot fight us. We shall not fail or falter."

"Why are you doing this?" said the Prime Minister.

"Let's face it, you are never going to take the conservation of the Earth, seriously. Even the staggering event of statues coming to life, will not be enough to shock you into doing the right things. Man, is a needy, selfish and often greedy creature, programmed to get want he wants, by force if necessary."

"You make it sound as though it's entirely our fault," said the Prime Minister.

"It was no different in my day. I suspect we would have behaved as you are now. However, we are not you, and we can do what you never will. This planet wants to survive and we are serious about surviving with it. It's our time now Prime Minister. The statues are taking over."

The Prime Minister sat on the edge of the bench with his head in his hands. This was something that films and books were made of, except, with what had happened over the last forty-eight hours, this too could be possible. He looked towards the double doors, hoping that some of his ministers would walk in and announce that the training exercise was over.

Churchill spoke again. There was a reassurance in his voice. "You need to make a statement, Prime Minister. You need to protect the people of London. They are relying on you. There must be no resistance, no military forces, and no covert plans. You cannot beat us."

The statue had already drawn up a prepared speech to be televised.

At this stage, the Prime Minister wasn't sure he could speak, let alone make a statement.

Molly was sitting once more on the marble table when she heard a door slam and muffled voices. She listened to stone on stone as the statue of Edith Cavell came back down the stairs.

"Let go of me," shouted a familiar voice, and her brother was shoved into the room. Molly ran to him and threw her arms around him, and he was just as overjoyed to see her. They turned together to face the statue in an act of defiance. Cavell spun round, ducked through the doorway and slammed the door shut behind her.

Molly told Charlie everything in detail. From finding the Tour Guide, the questioning of statues, and what he had told her about the Agalmata, to meeting Sherlock Holmes and the Coade stone Lion. Her daring climb under the bridge and the clue, her capture and the journey here. Even the bit about seeing him through the little window, arriving in the police car.

"Look, I'm sorry I wasn't there, when you, you know, last night," said Charlie.

"That's ok, you've been distracted."

Sounds as though you've had quite an adventure."

"There's more," said Molly. She explained what the statue had said about their father and the Agalmata.

Charlie remained silent until she had finished. "I don't think you should pay any attention to what the statue has said. You know Dad wouldn't do anything wrong, and besides he's not here to comment, so we shouldn't make any judgement."

"How do you explain how the statues know everything about me? Remember what I said after that business at the embassy?"

"I don't know Moll. Maybe there is some connection with you and statues? I met your Tour Guide, in fact that's how I ended up in here." Charlie explained the meeting. "Odd looking chap and I don't think you should trust him anymore, especially if he is part of this Agalmata. You should ask yourself how he manages to turn up every time."

"What do you mean?"

"Well, you said he was on the bridge when you were looking to meet Sherlock Holmes. Then he appeared out of nowhere when we were searching for you, and what was the meeting with Emmeline Pankhurst all about?"

"I'm not sure we should jump to any conclusions, about him either, he's been a friend of Mum and Dad's for years. Do you know he's our godfather?"

"Godfather? How did that happen? I didn't know we had a godfather. Anyhow, I think he's working for the statues and they're telling him what to do and where to go."

Molly knew it was a strong possibility. "I think he might be in trouble."

Charlie didn't reply.

"Anyway," said Molly. "What's happening with Amber? I thought you would have stayed at hers?"

"I was, but I came looking for you. Besides, I don't think Amber could have coped with all this."

Molly smiled.

Charlie scanned the room. "Especially considering that these marble slabs, makes me think this is an old mortuary."

Molly's smile disappeared. To think, she'd been lying down where dead people had been.

We're under Tower Bridge," Charlie continued, "and I know there's a place called Dead Man's Gate. It's where the river naturally eddies and any bodies in the Thames would have washed up here. It's likely that there would be a mortuary nearby to make things easier. Bodies would have been left here until someone claimed them."

"Why were there bodies in the Thames?" said Molly screwing up her face with the thought.

"Suicides, murders, they were not the best of times. Talking of dead people, you know what I don't understand is how the statue of Sherlock Holmes has come to life."

"Nor me."

"But you think he's been sent?"

"I think he's trying to help me."

"I suppose if you had to send a statue to help, you would want to send a statue you might trust. You're trusting Sherlock Holmes because he is different from the rest and maybe has a different agenda. So what about the clue?"

"The Hearted Pirate?" said Molly.

"Do you know what it means?" said Charlie.

"I've been trying to think. Are there any London pirates?" said Molly.

"Pirate radio stations?" Charlie shrugged. "London is a port and used to be the busiest, it would have attracted lots of pirates. They used to hang them at Execution Dock, which was at Wapping, about a mile down the river from here."

"I wondered if there was something missing. The Hearted Pirate," she repeated. "Shouldn't that be *the something* Hearted Pirate? Such as, The Cruel Hearted Pirate or the True Hearted Pirate?"

"I wonder why he left you a clue instead of just telling you out straight."

"I've thought about that, I think it might be this telepathy thing, he didn't want the rest of the statues to know."

"It could be an anagram of course." Charlie searched his pockets and pulled out a pencil and a piece of scrap paper. "The best way to solve anagrams is to write all the letters round in a circle. Dad taught me that." Charlie wrote them all out. There were a lot of letters.

"Think of an aim," said Charlie. "He was trying to tell you something, presumably useful, maybe something to do with conservation."

"Or how to stop the statues?"

"I can see heated, reheated and preheated, oh, and earth and radiate," said Charlie.

"How do you do that? All I can see is The Hearted Pirate." "Hatred, aerated, here's one for you, tetrahedra."

Molly frowned.

"It's a pyramid," said Charlie.

He was crossing out letters as he went. He searched for more pieces of scrap paper. "You haven't got your notepad have you?"

"No, the statue took my bag with everything in it."

"I've got threat and earthed."

"That sounds good."

"Yeah, but it leaves Pie."

Molly remembered she hadn't eaten all day.

Charlie burst out laughing. "Cracked it."

"Really?" said Molly, excitedly.

"Parade their teeth." That's their secret, get them all to show their teeth, and they'll die.

Molly laughed. She was so pleased that her brother was there, even if it did mean that he was in as much danger as she was

Like a school teacher checking on a class because of the noise, Cavell reappeared at the door

"It has begun," she said. "The battle for London."

"In what way?" said Charlie.

"The intention is not to harm. We are trusting that you will realise we can do better than you are doing now. Once we have demonstrated our control of London, we expect the rest of the world to follow suit."

"Don't you think that the people here might have something to say about that?" said Charlie.

"Why go against us, we can bring you development and evolution? We can prevent you from destroying yourselves."

"Yes, but at what price? To be ruled by statues? We won't agree to that," said Charlie.

"As we speak, statues are gathering in Trafalgar Square," said the statue. "Great leaders, statesmen, politicians, a wealth of skills and knowledge; there are many thousands of us in London alone. You cannot stop us. There is nothing we cannot do. Perhaps you would like to witness events from the top of this building?"

"No thanks," said Charlie. "We're quite happy in this mortuary."

"Suit yourselves." The statue climbed the stairs again.

"We got to get out of this place, Molly," said Charlie, once the statue was out of earshot. He walked over to the door the statue had just used. "This door's been left unlocked," he said.

"Yes, but the statue is between us and the outside."

"What about that door?" He strode over to the other door.

"That leads to the river. It's where I was brought in," said Molly.

Charlie put his shoulder against the door and gave it a shove. "It's solid but it's old. I wonder if we could burn it down. We'd need some tinder and kindling, just like lighting a fire in the jungle," said Charlie getting excited by the idea.

"And something to light it with," said Molly.

Charlie was already searching around at the end of the room.

"Careful back there," said Molly. "I heard rats earlier."

Charlie appeared with a pile of shredded, dry paper from one of the cardboard boxes.

"How are you going to light it?" Molly asked again.

Charlie patted his pockets.

With a low whoomf, the boiler at the back of the room fired to heat the water.

"Perfect," said Charlie. "It will have a pilot light." He walked over. "I'm going to need your necklace, please Molly, the Dammar will burn really well."

Molly reluctantly handed him the necklace, acknowledging it was good idea.

Charlie carried over a piece of lit, rolled paper from the boiler, and put it to the shredded paper at the bottom of the door. He added the small resin necklace, which immediately caught and burned with a steady flame, and some torn up strips of the cardboard box. The two of them continued to rummage for things to add to the fire, and in no time, a flame was licking its way up the door. They stood back and watched as the door blackened and burned. Molly felt her eyes sting and she coughed.

"There's a lot of smoke in here, Charlie," she said.

"The door must have been treated with some sort of wood preserve, it has really taken," said Charlie.

It had gone well up to this point, but now Molly doubted her brother's actions, he may have put them in more danger.

The room was filling with acrid smoke and sparks were flying off the door. It didn't look as though it was going to burn through in time; they'd have to leave the room.

Taking his sister's hand, Charlie opened the unlocked door to the stairs and pulled her upwards. The air from the stairwell fuelled the fire and more sparks flew off in different directions. The smoke followed them up the spiral staircase. Charlie looked through the small windows on each landing, looking for a way out, but they were all too small. At the top of the stairs was another wooden door. Charlie reached for the handle.

"Charlie, the statue will be behind there," warned Molly.

Charlie looked back down the stairs. The smoke had already filled half the stairwell.

"We can't stay here, it will be a death trap before long." He slowly opened the door. He was met by daylight, but no statue. Peering out, they could see that they were on the top of the abutment tower and a flat gangway, protected by ramparts, ran around a grey tiled sloping roof with windows in it. Charlie stepped out further. Strangely, the statue was nowhere to be seen.

Molly guessed that Cavell must be round the other side of the sloping roof. She followed Charlie out and together they looked over the ramparts. There was nothing but the road over the bridge and the river underneath. It was then they heard and felt the footsteps of the statue returning towards them.

"Quick, this way," whispered Charlie.

Like fugitives, the two of them silently ran to the next corner of the sloping roof, crouching as they moved. Charlie peered round the next corner; it was all clear, so they moved forward. In theory, they could keep on creeping round like this, from corner to corner, until help arrived, like a thrilling game of hide and seek. They glanced back once more.

"The door." Molly gasped. "We've left the door open!"

Charlie shifted his position.

"Don't," said Molly, sensing he was going to make a run for it. "You'll never make it."

The statue stepped into view, and the two of them ducked back.

Molly felt herself trembling. It was cold this high up, but she also felt exposed and vulnerable. She gripped her brother's hand.

Charlie sneaked a cautious look around the corner again. He watched as the statue of Cavell stood in front of the open door, turning its head to one side as if studying the grain in the wood. It then pushed the door closed and locked it. The statue knew. It turned around to face where they were hiding. Charlie dropped back out of sight. They were trapped.

"Where do you think you can run to, children?" There was menace in the statue's voice.

They could keep running round the walkway, although they had no idea how quickly the statue could move, and was help actually coming? Molly and Charlie moved to the ramparts and looked over once more. On this side was a narrow shelf, which ran right around the top and led to wide metal struts, the anchor ties that led down towards the ground. A stone gargoyle sat over each of the four struts, one in each corner.

Charlie looked at his sister. "We've no choice Molly."

Molly nodded. After Westminster Bridge, she could do anything.

Charlie swung himself up onto the rampart and then over onto the ledge. He turned to face back into the stonework and looked at Molly.

"The ledge feels solid enough," he said to reassure her. Molly nodded, confident that this was their way out.

Charlie shuffled along so that Molly could get onto the ledge with him. She took hold of the top of the ramparts and heaved herself up, swinging a leg over, followed by her other leg, and she was then standing on the narrow, stone ledge. She gripped the top of the stone rampart, and as she was already cold, the exposed position was making her hands go numb.

She looked down.

It was a long way. If she let go now, she would fall through the cold air for about a second, twisting a little, arms beating the air, eyes wide open, before hitting the tarmac. She could see herself striking the ground. She would die and it would be horribly painful. In that instant, Molly had visualised the whole falling thing. She turned back to focus on something else. She swallowed, her saliva had a sickly taste to it.

Charlie had continued to shuffle along the ledge and was now at the stone gargoyle. "Let's just hope this doesn't come alive," he muttered. He stepped onto the back of the gargoyle without opposition, then turned back to his sister.

"Come on Moll, it's easy," he said.

Molly was ready to be sick. "I can't move," she said. Completely gripped by fear, she couldn't help looking again at the tarmac below.

"Let's go back," she pleaded. "The statue hasn't hurt us so far, why should it?" She was reasoning out their surrender.

"Molly!" Charlie shouted. "The statue!"

Molly looked. Edith Cavell was coming for her and she didn't look like she was ready to negotiate any surrender.

It was enough to make Molly move.

The statue got to the rampart and reached out to grab her. Molly ducked to avoid the stone hand but in doing so her foot slipped off the ledge and one hand loosened its grip. Off balance, she twisted to compensate — and sensed herself beginning to fall. Charlie stared, horrified.

With absolute commitment, Molly pushed and jumped, turning her body in mid air, her arms out stretched. Fingers extended, her hands searching for safety.

She found it in the head and neck of the stone gargoyle and she threw her arms around it leaving her feet swinging in cold air.

Charlie immediately clamped both his hands over the top of Molly's, so that she could not let go of the gargoyle. There was now the weight of both of them resting on this ancient piece of stone. It had to hold.

"I'm OK," said Molly. Her legs kicked as if on an imaginary bicycle. "Keep going, I can pull myself up."

Reluctant to let go, Charlie waited for Molly to get a foothold and then reached across to the metal suspension strut, keen to relieve some of the burden on the gargoyle. With a fully extended leg and arm, he gained the pale blue coloured metal and climbed on.

Molly stared into the eyes of the gargoyle as she pulled herself up. "I do hope you're made of Coade stone," she said. Hooking a leg over one of its wings, Molly swivelled herself onto the back of the gargoyle.

The statue of Cavell was still reaching out but Molly was too far away. She grinned at the statue, knowing that it couldn't follow her. Cavell looked around for an improvisation, and then grabbed one of the castellations between her two stone hands. With a shove and a sharp twist, she broke it off and lifted the large chunk of stonework above her head. She threw it.

Molly cried out and instinctively closed her eyes.

The piece fell short, curved in mid air, then accelerated to the ground, exploding into hundreds of pieces on the tarmac below. Molly stared at the shattered debris. That could have been her.

Charlie was now on the metal support and he reached out for Molly to join him. Now, without hesitation, she took her brother's hand and stepped across. Once on, the two of them sat astride the metal struts and started to shuffle themselves down its angled length. The wide metal dug into the inside of Molly's thighs but this was infinitely better than being on that ledge. This was escape.

There was a wail of sirens in the background from police cars and fire engines as they raced towards Tower Bridge.

"Is that for us?" shouted Molly.

"Think so," Charlie shouted back. "Look behind you, it's the fire we started."

Molly looked back up to the ramparts. Thick black smoke was pluming out of the far side of the tower. Edith Cavell had gone.

Once Molly and Charlie were on safe ground, the police had a number of questions for them. An ambulance had arrived and they were both wrapped in warm blankets and someone had supplied cups of tea. Molly felt herself trembling, unsure if it was the cold or emotion.

Armed police officers had entered the gatehouse but Edith Cavell had not been found. Molly told them about the barge and the police went to look down by the river as well as alerting their colleagues who worked on the Thames.

"I've been trying to tell everyone that the statues were bad," said Molly to the woman police officer. "I've always said they're not who they say they are."

Molly described the conversations she had had with the statue of Cavell. "It's all to do with Eleanor Coade and the Lion, Sherlock Holmes told me. I think I've discovered their weakness. You have to shoot them twice, or burn them twice to destroy them."

As far as the police officer was concerned, Molly was babbling, probably delirious and suffering from shock. She took a report all the same.

"Look," said the officer, "I'm not sure if we can prosecute a statue, and as we are really stretched at the moment, I'll have to take a detailed statement from you another time. I want you both to go straight home to your parents. Is that understood?"

Molly and Charlie solemnly agreed. They then set off immediately for Trafalgar Square.

Boudicca reined the horses to a halt. They were panting and had it been physically possible, they would have been sweating profusely. They had been driven hard, but they were the sort of horses that could take it.

Boudicca stepped off the back of the chariot, she knew she was trapped. Just as they had reached the top of Regent Street and Oxford Circus, three buses had been driven across the mouth of the junction, blocking it from building to building. Boudicca had turned hard, almost on the spot; one of the advantages of driving this type of two wheeled chariot, and headed back the way they had come. Other vehicles were being placed across the side streets. A refuse lorry, a Luton van with tail-lift, and a digger truck had all been commandeered by the police. Even before she got to the other end of the street, she knew that they would have sealed that as well. Armed police officers were taking up positions at all the road blocks.

That didn't mean she had given up. Holding her spear with both hands, she rammed it at a shop window. One of the large plate glass display windows shattered. Her daughters grinned. This was their mother of old. In went another window, and Boudicca was showered with thick heavy glass to which she was impervious. The shop was a gentleman's outfitters. The daughters joined their mother and ransacked the display, throwing out expensive, fine quality suits. Another shop window was smashed, then another. Each time the contents were thrown out onto the pavement. Sports gear and equipment, televisions and cameras, jeans and fashion wear lay strewn across the road. Last time they did this here in London, they sacked and burned the town, killed all the Romans and their sympathisers. There was a temptation to do that again, today.

The police looked on. The cost was going to be astronomical but for the time being, they had contained her.

.

The Prime Minister had called an emergency meeting with his senior staff. He was just waiting for everyone to arrive when his secretary buzzed him.

"Sir Anthony is here," she said. "He needs to see you immediately, Prime Minister."

The head of MI5 entered the P.M.'s office, and came straight to the point. "We've uncovered something that suggests some of your ministers are in communication with someone outside of government. An organisation that call themselves the Agalmata. We also think the statues are plotting a takeover and are being assisted."

The Prime Minister wanted to swear. "I could have done with this information earlier Anthony. Do you know who?"

The head of MI5 gave him the details. "The good news is that none of your senior staff are involved," said Sir Anthony. "We have however, some suspicions about the Commissioner."

"The Commissioner, surely not?"

The secretary buzzed again to announce that everyone had arrived for the meeting.

"I'll be right there," said the Prime Minister. "You'd better come with me," he said to the head of MI5.

The two men stepped into one of the three conference rooms adjoining the Prime Minister's office. The PM's senior staff were all assembled, and were watching a large-screen television showing a mass evacuation of people. There were images of panic, confusion; some fighting had broken out. There was lots of congestion. The face of a young man appeared on the screen in high definition. He had cropped hair, several piercings in his nose and ears, and horrible looking teeth.

"Get out of London, man," he shouted shoving his face in to the camera. "It's the end. They're gonna turn us all to stone."

"Right then," said the Prime Minister. "Turn that idiot off and brief me on what's happening out there."

He would tell them of Churchill's ultimatum in a moment and besides, he had instructed someone to contact Thames Water for their assessment, and was waiting for a response.

The Home Secretary gave a summary. "The statues are still congregating in Trafalgar Square. We are sealing off the area and evacuating the square. The police have had reports of looting, damage and cars being set on fire in several different areas."

"How serious?" said the Prime Minister.

"Fairly substantial damage in some areas, minor injuries, some police. Arrests have been made."

"Arrests?"

"We're getting reports that the statues are not involved in all of these disturbances. Opportunists using the moment to cause chaos. We are waiting for more information."

"As if I haven't got enough to deal with," said the Prime Minister.

"The good news," continued the Home Secretary, "we've contained Boudicca. She's in Regent Street in a roadblock. She is currently smashing shop windows, but at least she's no longer mobile."

"What about the reports this morning on the missing girl, believed to have been abducted by a statue?"

"Rescued. She was in Tower Bridge, not the Tower of London, along with her brother. They've described Edith Cavell, who seems to have escaped."

One of the junior ministers entered the room and the PM held up his hand for silence, and to allow the minister to speak.

"We've spoken to Thames Water, at their headquarters in Reading, they've tried to contact each of their plants without success; they've sent staff, but I think we can assume the threat is genuine," explained the minister.

It was the Prime Minister's turn now to brief his staff. He filled them in with the details, the Head of MI5's findings, and Churchill's threats.

"He's going to release the virus unless we surrender to the statues," said the Prime Minister.

The news was baffling, galling, and preposterous. Some expressed that it felt as though they had been beaten before they knew they were under attack.

"We need to fight back," said the Home Secretary. "Do we know where Myddelton, Jenner and Faraday are now?"

No one knew, they hadn't been seen all morning.

"Are we considering evacuation?" said the Home Secretary.

"Impossible, in the time frame" said the Prime Minister. "We all appreciate how difficult it would be, and where would we start?"

"What about using the police to take control," said one of the ministers directing his comment directly at the Home Secretary.

"I'm not sure they have the resources. They're stretched as it is," said the Home Secretary.

"Then why have we allowed the statues to congregate in Trafalgar

Square?" said the same minister. "They look as though they are gathering forces."

The Prime Minister remembered it had been the Commissioner who had suggested that they allow that; easier to monitor them, he'd said.

"We need the army," someone else suggested.

"Churchill has insisted no military or he'll release the virus," said the Prime Minister.

"Then we need to do it covertly," said the Secretary of State. "Alert the SAS, get them into the City and destroy these things."

The Prime Minister considered the suggestion, then turned to the Defence Minister. "Make some calls."

Sir Walter Raleigh may have felt he was getting a bit of a raw deal. He had once sat in the middle of Whitehall, outside the Ministry of Defence, on a lawn named after him. He had been comfortable there since 1959, but then in 2001, they moved him. Still dressed in the familiar clothing of his time, as governed by his social position, he now stood at his new home outside the Greenwich Visitors' Centre.

A very long walk into town.

On top of all that, he had been taking a lot of stick over cigarettes and potato crisps. He was heading for Trafalgar Square as instructed. Attempting to be discreet, he stuck to seldom used paths and back-alleys and even the occasional sewer or underground tunnel. Lots had changed, of course, since his day.

He had just reached the New Kent Road, by Elephant and Castle, when walking towards him wearing England shirts and carrying cans of beer, were four well-built lads.

"En-ger-land," shouted one of them as the others clapped in unison, raising their hands above their heads. The lads had been in town looking for talking statues. Unable to get anywhere near them because of the crowds, they'd hit the pubs. They blocked the path of the oncoming statue.

"Hey, hey, lads, what have we got 'ere then?" said one of them.

"Awright mate, where'd you fink you're off to?" said another.

The third took a long slurp from his beer can. "Where did you get that hat, where did you get that hat?"

Everyone laughed.

Everyone, except Raleigh.

"Come on my son, get with it," said the first lad again, as he stepped forward and with his right hand, gave Sir Walter Raleigh a couple of friendly slaps to his left cheek.

With the skill of an experienced military man, Raleigh lifted his sword, a swept-hilt rapier, and drove it through the man's chest. The sword went straight through and out the other side. He held the man upright on the sword, easily taking the weight.

The others froze in horror and amazement. Someone dropped a beer can, which foamed on the pavement.

Raleigh looked down the length of his sword. "Not as good as my original sword, but all things considered, not bad," he said. There was a sucking sound as he pulled the sword from the man's body, and the corpse dropped to the pavement. Raleigh bent over, wiped his sword on the dead man's jacket, and walked on unimpeded. This wouldn't have happened if he hadn't had to come so far.

The statue of Raleigh continued to Waterloo Bridge, where his presence brought traffic to a standstill. He glanced over and admired the River Thames, which seemed a lot cleaner now than it had in his day, and he took pleasure in the sights of London from both sides of the bridge. The place had both changed and remained the same. It had been an arduous hike from Greenwich, but not without interest.

He saw the police cars at the far end of the bridge and police running up between stationary cars. A trap perhaps, but what could they do?

Raleigh had almost crossed the bridge, when the shouting started. Armed police officers, an armoured vehicle, and even a helicopter overhead. He was being told to lie down on the ground — as if.

Between walking and jogging, Molly and Charlie had covered the ground quickly. They had stayed with the river, with a few twists and turns, alleyways and underpasses. They were now on Embankment and it occurred to Molly to stop at Temple Gardens and call in on the educationalist, Forster. She was ready to give him a mouthful, now that Charlie was with her. They spotted the action on Waterloo Bridge as a police helicopter did impressive nose-down turns.

"Come on," said Charlie as he accelerated into a run. "Let's see what's happening."

They reached the steps that led onto the bridge, and were promptly stopped by a uniformed Police Community Support Officer. Molly read this fact from the badge on his fluorescent jacket.

"Hold it you two, you can't go up there, the road is closed."

"What's happening?" said Charlie.

"Police matter, you'll have to go round," said the officer.

"Is it to do with the statues?" said Molly.

"Yes," said the officer. "Walter Raleigh has killed a man at Elephant and Castle."

Molly and Charlie looked at each other. Now this was serious.

"Stabbed him with a sword, he did," added the officer, probably giving away more information than he should have done. "We are just trying to arrest him and—"

The officer didn't finish his sentence. There were several loud cracks and all three of them flinched.

"Gun," said the officer.

"They're shooting at him?" said Charlie. "But he's made of metal."

Two more shots were heard, this time much louder as if more powerful.

Up on the bridge, the statue of Raleigh had refused to stop, lie down or even pass the time of day. Two officers had approached him from behind a bulletproof shield, strong enough to stop his sword. The statue stood there, bemused. He allowed them to approach and to get close enough to use a Taser on him. He'd never seen one before but knew it worked on firing two thin copper wires that carried 50,000 volts of electricity. A warning was shouted, and then the weapon was fired. What a curious, modern world we now live in, thought the statue.

Of course, the Taser had no effect.

The statue kicked out at the bulletproof shield, the force breaking the wrist of the officer holding it. Raleigh lifted his sword, stepped, and made a feint to the left with a circular deception, and then a thrust to the right. The tip of his sword was now pressing on the Adam's apple of the second officer, who dropped his spent Taser and tried not to swallow.

An instruction was given over the police radio. One of the armed police officers fired two rounds from his Heckler and Koch MP5, into Raleigh's chest. The rounds ricocheted away. Another officer with a G36 fired a single 5.56 millimetre round that travelled at 920 metres per second. The round hit Raleigh directly over where his heart should be. The power behind the shot rocked the statue, and penetrated the metal, but apart from that, it hadn't altered his day.

"I can help," said Molly, desperate to see what was going on. "Sherlock Holmes left me a clue underneath Westminster Bridge; it's all to do with the Coade stone Lion. You have to shoot the statues twice."

"I think they've done that Moll," said her brother.

The officer looked sceptical at this fifteen year old, and the nonsense pouring out of her.

"Then fire. Fire them twice. As in set light to them twice." As she said this, she knew she wasn't making any sense.

The officer was listening to his radio. He put his fingers to his earpiece, pushing it in tighter. "Officers injured," he said, turning to run up the steps. This seemed to conflict with his original instructions to guard the bridge, and for a moment, he was caught, hopping from one foot to another.

"Look Molly, we can't do any good here," said Charlie. "Besides it sounds too dangerous up there. Let's go and see what's happening at Trafalgar."

Molly nodded. Another battle, no doubt.

The two of them carried on along Victoria Embankment. They hadn't gone far when there was a honking of a car horn. Molly turned to see a black Range Rover pulling up against the far side kerb. The driver's door was being opened while the car was still coming to a stop, and a man stepped out. He was tall, in a dark suit and with short, neatly cut hair. He put his right hand in the air and shouted across the traffic. "Molly, Charlie, wait up."

Molly and Charlie both slowed to a walk.

The driver dodged the cars as he crossed the road and stepped onto the pavement. He approached them with his arms outstretched and in a slightly stooped position, as if trying to gather a yard full of chickens.

"Thank goodness I found you," he said.

Molly had no idea who he was, but he look friendly enough. "You're parents have sent me," said the driver.

"What?" said Molly. "Where are they?"

"They're in hiding. They want you to come with me so I can take you to them," said the driver.

"They phoned the house," said Charlie turning to his sister. "I forgot to tell you. They said we were in danger and not to go out."

"Yes," said the driver. "Yes, that's right, you are in danger. Come with me now, both of you." He waved his left hand in the direction of the waiting car.

"Why are they in hiding? Why didn't they come and get us?" said Molly. She was looking towards the parked car as she spoke. A front seat passenger was staring out of his window towards the river. Molly thought it odd that he wasn't looking in their direction.

"It's to do with the Agalmata," said the driver.

Molly turned to look at him. "What about the Agalmata?"

"It's not safe to talk about them here," said the driver. "You're parents can do all that. It's not far."

"How do you know them?" said Molly. "Who are you?" She looked back towards the car but the driver had now positioned himself between her and a view of the vehicle.

"I've known your parents for years, we're good friends. Look, I know this is difficult for you, but they have asked me to bring you to them."

"Come on Molly," said Charlie. "Dad will be able to sort all this out." He stepped towards the road. "When did Mum and Dad get back in the country?" he asked the driver.

"This morning," said the driver as he turned and walked with Charlie to the kerb. "They tried to get hold of you, but I suppose with all the phones not working, they could only leave a message. They took the first flight they could."

Charlie and the driver started to cross the road forcing Molly to follow in order to hear what was being said. She looked at the car again. The front seat passenger was still looking in the opposite direction. She wondered why the driver, and not the passenger had got out, which would have been safer.

"What made them come back?" said Charlie. "How did they find out about the statues?"

"The whole world knows about the statues," said the driver.

The traffic had slowed, allowing the three of them to cross at a leisurely trot. They were half way when Molly thought there was something familiar about the man in the car. She couldn't quite place him, but it was recent.

"It will be great to see them," said Charlie. "This is all so crazy." He turned to speak to Molly who was still walking just behind. "Won't it be great see them? Dad will explain everything. You'll see."

They were about ten paces from the car.

"How did you find us?" said Charlie to the driver.

Eight paces from the car.

"Luck more than anything, we've been looking all over," said the driver.

Six paces from the car.

We were captured by a statue, and held in Tower Bridge," said Charlie.

Four paces.

"Yes, we know," said the driver.

Two paces.

"We started a fire and then climbed down the metal arms of the bridge," said Charlie.

They reached the car.

"Really," said the driver as he opened the door of the car inviting Charlie to get in.

Molly recognised the passenger. The last time she'd seen him was on a shingle beach. He had been wearing a blue woollen hat, overalls, headphones, and using a metal detector.

Charlie was easing himself into the back seat.

"Estamos en peligro. No consiga en el coche," said Molly in Spanish.

We're in danger. Don't get in the car.

Charlie stopped with his right hand on the top of the open car door and his left leg in the car.

"¿Cómo lo sabe?" asked Charlie looking past the driver at his sister. *How do you know?"*

"Reconozco al oltro hombre en el coche, él es malo." *I recognise the other man in the car, he is bad.*

The driver turned to look at Molly. She could see in his eyes that they were now in trouble.

"Run!" she shouted as she pulled away from the car.

"Oh no you don't," said the driver as he reached out and grabbed Molly by her hair. At the same time, he kicked the passenger door smashing it into Charlie's right leg.

Molly heard her brother cry out. She lost sight of him as her head was pulled down towards the ground. She was outraged at someone pulling her hair, and the pain made her eyes water. She heard a car door opening and knew it would be the passenger. Any second he'd be round the car and helping the driver. She swung out with clenched fists but couldn't make contact with anything. Someone was behind her. Her arms were being pinned to her sides.

"Hold her," said the driver as he turned and kicked the car door again, slamming it into Charlie, who was bent over clutching his leg. Charlie cried out as his body took most of the blow. The driver opened the car door and started to push Charlie inside.

Molly knew she had to do something. They hadn't just had a daring escape from Cavell, only to fall into the hands of the Agalmata. The man holding her arms, was strong; Molly had felt his grip before and knew she wouldn't be able to break free.

"Hey! You!"

"Someone was shouting from across the road, and Molly twisted to see.

It was the Police Community Support Officer they'd met on the bridge. He was stepping into the road with his left hand outstretched to stop the traffic while holding his radio in his right hand.

"What's going on?" said the officer as he approached. The traffic on their side of the road had come to a stop.

The driver stepped forward to meet the officer.

"It's all right," he said. "We're police officers. We're detectives, and these people are under arrest."

What nonsense thought Molly, but she could she see that the officer was already beginning to relax as he accepted the explanation.

It was now or never.

Molly slammed her head backwards and connected with the breastbone of the man holding her. At the same time, she turned and drove her knee into his groin. He cried out and released her instantly. Molly wrenched the rear car door open and pulled her brother's arm, helping him to his feet. The officer and the driver were beginning to react and Molly knew they had just seconds to get away.

"Help us," she shouted. "They're kidnapping us."

"What?" said the officer.

With that, the driver turned again to face the officer, and with a flat open hand struck out at the officer's throat. The officer fell to his knees without any sound.

A car in the traffic sounded its horn, and the driver of another was getting out. Molly and Charlie were clear of the door and already skirting round the back of the car and onto the pavement.

"Come on, Charlie," said Molly. "We've got to run."

Charlie's legs started to work, and brother and sister broke into a trot, then a run as they supported each other. Molly didn't look back. They kept on running, crossing the road further on and then into a side street. They stopped in a small yard and hid behind two huge refuse bins.

Charlie looked at his sister and then bent down to pull up his trouser leg. He examined the red crease across the bottom of his leg. The blood had come to the surface but the skin was intact.

"You all right?" said Molly.

"Well, I don't think it's broken," said Charlie. "Who were they?"

"Agalmata, I'm sure of it. The man in the passenger seat was the man who grabbed me when I tried to get away from Cavell. She said he was helping them."

"Do you think they've got Mum and Dad."

Molly thought for a moment. "Somehow, I don't think so. You said there was a message from them on the answer phone. Was that from yesterday?"

"Yeah," said Charlie.

"Assuming they've got an evening flight from Lima, they would have to change at Madrid or somewhere in the States. They wouldn't be here yet."

"Did you hear that man say they were police? To that officer. I do hope he's ok," said Molly.

"What do we do now?" said Charlie.

"I think we've lost them," said Molly as she took a quick peek around one of the refuse bins. I suppose we carry on to Trafalgar Square."

Molly checked a couple more times for the black car or its occupants. They then cautiously crept out and carried on through the back streets, and arrived at Strand. The place was heaving. There was a surge of people coming towards them, away from Trafalgar Square, whose passage was being hampered by parked motorcycles and cars as well as a long line of police vans.

Molly and Charlie pushed their way up the road, trying not to become separated, ignoring comments from the crowd that they were going the wrong way. As they reached Trafalgar Square, it became obvious that the police were evacuating the area. Barriers were going up, and announcements to leave in an orderly fashion were being given over loudhailers.

Standing above the departing crowd, Molly could see the usual statues still on their plinths but now alive and moving. Sir Henry Havelock and Sir Charles Napier, and towards the back on horseback, George IV who curiously had a pigeon on his head, which he hadn't bothered to brush away. The statues of James II and George Washington were standing on the steps leading up to the National Gallery. There was gathering of other statues in the centre of the square, just as Edith Cavell had said there would be. Trafalgar Square had seen some demonstrations in its past but nothing quite like this; London was now a very different place.

Molly and Charlie were finding it increasingly difficult to move forward as the mass of people, being driven by a fan of advancing police officers, was pushing them further and further back. Molly sensed, more than heard, that someone was calling her name. She turned to her left, then to her right. There it was again. Then Charlie heard it.

"Did you hear that? Someone's calling you," said Charlie.

Molly skipped and jumped trying to gain height and a better view. She was then blocked by an officer in a yellow jacket.

"Keep moving please," said the police officer. "Keep going."

Molly stood firm while still trying to find who was calling her.

"Come miss, you can't stay here, the Square is closed."

"I'm looking for someone," she said.

"I'm not bothered," said the officer. "You have to leave."

Molly spotted movement. It was to the left and high up above the officer, a man standing on a balcony, waving his arms above his head.

"There," she pointed. "It's my grandfather, on that balcony, he lives there." The officer turned and looked in the direction of Molly's outstretched finger. She was pointing at a narrow building that said Uganda House in big letters on the front of the building. There was a big man with white hair on the top balcony. The officer could hear him shouting.

Charlie looked up and not sure, whispered to Molly, "Who's that?"

Molly threw him a look. "Can we go to him, please officer? He will be quite worried on his own."

The police officer let them through with instruction to stay indoors. The man on the balcony was now pointing to the entrance directly below him on street level and Molly could see that Uganda House had a shop window, and to the left, a glass door. They pushed their way through the surge of exiting people.

Waiting for them, behind the glass door, was Gee-Gee.

"That's the Tour Guide," said Charlie.

"Yes," said Molly.

"Molly," said Charlie catching hold of her arm. "I'm not sure this is such a good idea. He's working for the statues?"

"Then we need to know why."

"He sent me to get captured."

"And just as well he did, otherwise I'd still be in there. Look, by going in we can put all this to him, and he's our only source on what is actually going on."

They reached the glass door, and a dark skinned man in a shirt and tie, unlocked the door and welcomed them in, and then immediately relocked the door.

"What are you doing in here?" said Molly to Gee-Gee.

"Watching the spectacle, just like the rest of the world," he said.

"What is this place?"

"The Ugandan High Commission, it's where you would come if you wanted a visa to go to Uganda, amongst other things. This is Ochen," Gee-Gee introduced the man who had let them in. "He is from Uganda. Everyone in the building has left, leaving Ochen to mind the shop."

Ochen's shirt was too big for him, especially around the collar. "Welcome, welcome," said Ochen, smiling, nodding, and shaking hands with the new arrivals in a well-practised manner. He seemed pleased to see them, and Molly guessed that he probably would sooner have company than be on his own.

"I met Ochen from when I used to work here as a tour guide. We used to have a crafty cigarette together out the back." Gee-Gee checked with Ochen that it was all right to take his guests upstairs. "Come on," said Gee-Gee. "It's all happening outside and we've got ringside seats."

He led them out of the reception area, into a wide corridor, and up a marble staircase that zigzagged between floors. Although the building had been modernised, it was still old and as they trotted up the steps, there was a hollow echo all around them.

Charlie looked at Molly questioning whether she knew what she was doing.

Molly knew exactly what her brother was trying to say. Gee-Gee hadn't mentioned anything about her imprisonment, nor that he had met Charlie and sent him to Tower Bridge, and his capture by Cavell. He hadn't even asked how they'd escaped.

She silenced Charlie with a finger to her lips.

They reached the top after three double flights and entered one of the offices to see desks, computers, telephones, with paperwork strewn everywhere; the office staff had apparently left in some haste.

Gee-Gee walked across to an open window that gave access to a balcony. He was about to climb out when Molly said, "Gee-Gee."

He stopped and turned.

"Before we go outside, I think you have some explaining to do."

Gee-Gee looked captured. "About what?"

"About how you set me up, sending me to Tower Bridge for a view, and I got taken by the statue of Edith Cavell," said Charlie. "We were bloody lucky to escape and could easily have been killed."

"And how did you know I was on Westminster Bridge yesterday?" said

Molly.

"And that I would be at the Tower of London this morning?" said Charlie. "Who's telling you where to go?"

"Now you're here with ringside seats, as you put it," said Molly. "Are you helping the statues? Are you in with them?"

Gee-Gee sat down on an office chair. He placed his hands on his knees and his big hung down towards his chest. He stared at the floor.

"We want the truth now, Gee-Gee," said Molly. "We want to know about the Agalmata. Is my dad involved?"

The last question brought Gee-Gee's head up as if it had hit a nerve. He didn't immediately say anything as though searching for the right words.

"When you were very young, and you weren't much older," he said turning to Charlie, "we were all together in Central America. "You, me, your dad and mum. Your dad and I were working together. You, Molly, got sick, very sick, and it didn't look as though you would pull through. You were in hospital, and the doctors put it down to an unknown jungle fever. They said they had tried everything, but there seemed nothing else they could do. They were looking to repatriate the whole family but it wasn't certain that you would survive the journey. Then we were intro-duced to a local Mayan villager who said he could cure you but he wanted something in return. He said that one day, the Earth would turn against the people for what they had done to the forest. Of course, your dad agreed, he would have agreed to anything, even though it didn't make sense." Gee-Gee turned to look out of the window.

This was all new to Molly. "He cured me?" she said.

"Yes, he cured you, well we think so. He blessed you, with a small, hand-carved statue, which he rested on your body and claimed it would connect you with another world. We kidded ourselves sometime afterwards that it was all nonsense, and you just got well. I don't think that now."

Molly looked at Charlie to see if he had any recognition of any of this.

"Nothing much happened when we came back to the UK," said Gee-Gee. "We settled back into work here, and every now and again, we were asked to do something by someone who referred to what had happened during that trip. There was no mention of the Agalmata, that came later, but it started to feel like a sort of club, a club where you could get things done because of the contacts. Your Dad wasn't happy, and he wanted to withdraw from them, and they seemed ok with that, but I got more and more involved. I wanted to know more about them, who and why, what was going to happen. I was warned, but persisted, and then tried to expose them to get answers.

"What do they want?" said Molly.

"The Agalmata or the statues?" said Gee-Gee.

"Well, both," said Molly.

"When you came to me, I'd had nothing to do with the Agalmata for some time. The university wasn't the only one to throw me out when I started meddling, the Agalmata did as well. My career and reputation went south. When the statues came alive, I felt vindicated but for what? We then spoke with Sir Francis Bacon who reminded me of the commitment we'd made to the Agalmata and your dad's promise, and I was sent to see Pankhurst, she must be leading what's happening on the ground, and she made it clear that if I didn't do what they wanted ..."

"Yes," said Molly.

Gee-Gee looked at Molly and Charlie in turn. "They would claim back the life that was saved."

Molly was working it out.

"That's you, Molly," said Charlie as he looked at Gee-Gee for confirmation.

"Gee-Gee nodded.

"What, kill me?" said Molly.

Gee-Gee shrugged. "I believe the Agalmata are capable of it, the statues certainly could. How could I take any chances? Besides, all they wanted was to keep you out of the way. I'm really sorry."

"What's going to happen now?" said Molly.

"Well, it's all out there. It's for the authorities now, perhaps they'll bring in the army," said Gee-Gee.

"Do the statues know we are here?" said Charlie.

"I don't think so," said Gee-Gee. "Ochen will keep the door locked and there's police everywhere."

Charlie looked at his sister. "Shall we go and have a look," he said, nodding towards the open window.

They all climbed out of the window and onto a narrow balcony. The windows had green lead flashing around them and were part of a grey slate tiled roof. All of it looked old and in need of some repair, and Molly was not happy about being up high again. The pale stone had that look of crumbling away just when you didn't need it to. She held back, and not just because of the poor masonry, she had no intention of being seen by the statues.

"My God," said Charlie looking over the edge. "What on earth is happening?"

"You know what this is? said Gee-Gee. "This is a show of strength."

The three of them surveyed the scene. There were statues everywhere; it was the most bizarre scene ever. Some statues were standing chatting, presumably having not seen each other since their deaths, and now making up for lost time. Some statues on horseback were riding up and down in front of the mounted police, and Lord Wellington on his horse, Copenhagen, was doing some dressage, and appeared to be taunting the police. Other statues, mainly military, appeared to be waiting for something to start. Richard I, the Lionheart, was waving his sword above his head, and General Wolfe and Earl Kitchener of Khartoum, both identified by Gee-Gee, looked ready for a fight.

Molly realised how difficult it was to recognise them when they were not on a plinth marked with their name.

"Will the lions come alive?" Charlie nodded at the statues of lions around Nelson's column.

"Well, technically I suppose they could," said Gee-Gee. "They were modelled on a real lion that died while the sculptor, Sir Edwin Landseer, was still working. He had to do a rushed job as the carcass was decaying."

"Nice," said Molly.

There were few people left in Trafalgar Square, but plenty still in all the adjoining streets. Even the reporters and TV crews had been moved out, although Molly could see that, like the three of them, many had gained access to rooftops and balconies. More statues were arriving, and it appeared that the police were either happy to have them all in one place or, more likely, were powerless to do anything about it.

Molly looked up at Nelson who was moving about on the top of his column, quite precariously at times.

"I don't suppose he can get down," said Gee-Gee.

"I don't think he needs to," said Charlie. "He appears to be acting as look-out."

"The police should stop them gathering like this," said Molly. "Soon we'll have every statue in London here. Then what will they do?"

"How can they stop them?" said Charlie. "We saw what little effect they had on stopping Sir Walter Raleigh, and he's here now, I've just seen him talking to Queen Elizabeth the First."

"What do you think they're going to do?" said Molly.

"Whatever their plans, it won't be good for London," said Charlie.

More police were arriving, many in riot gear, helmets and carrying shields. A pantechnicon, which had the words POLICE and INCIDENT CARAVAN on both sides, was manoeuvring across the entrance of Northumberland Avenue. On its roof were a number of antennae, flood-lights and CCTV cameras. Most of the adjoining roads to Trafalgar Square had a long lines of parked police vans.

Molly watched as two men in plain clothes stepped out of the incident caravan and walked towards the plinth of Charles I, who had already va-cated his position. They were joined by four officers in black clothing, two were armed and two were carrying short, ballistic shields, and they formed a box around the two detectives.

"Who do you think that is?" said Molly. They watched as the box approached a statue, and they started talking.

"That's Emmeline Pankhurst!" said Molly. "Gee-Gee, what's going on?"

"Honestly, I don't know," said Gee-Gee. "The two men might be negotiators."

Something else was happening to the left of one of the fountains; a noise, a scuffle, a statue was trying to pull another from his horse.

"That's Cromwell and Charles the first," said Gee-Gee. "They were against each other during the English Civil War."

Other statues were gathering around them. Some cheered, some pushed, it looked like a fight was about to start.

"Cromwell signed the death warrant for Charles the first," said Gee-Gee. "This might get ugly."

Charles I was using the rear of his horse to swing round into Cromwell. A line of police officers started to push their way from the outside of Trafalgar Square towards the two statues. They carried long batons and shields, and were wearing blue helmets all with the same number on the back. As they moved forward, some statues blocked their path and some officers struck out with their batons. A second, smaller group of armed officers, walking in a tight group, followed the line with their weapons held high ready for use. The first of the officers arrived at the fight and shouted instructions. Other statues were shouting and the level of noise was increasing throughout the square.

"They're going to get surrounded," shouted Charlie. "The police have been drawn in."

An officer was on the ground having been struck, then a second and third. They didn't appear to be seriously injured but their colleagues were forming a protective ring around them. Charles and Cromwell were no longer fighting, but had joined the other statues in attacking the police. Then, at the far side of Trafalgar Square, a statue had flipped over a police car, another statue was doing the same to a second vehicle, and another group of riot police were hurrying forward towards them. Some statues near to the steps leading up to the National Galley, were tearing off chunks of masonry and piling them up. Their strength was staggering.

Gunshot — two shots, then another two shots as the armed police officers fired at Cromwell. He was bullet-proof, and continued to advance on the police. What looked like hundreds of police officers poured out from the lines of parked vans, and moved quickly to strategic points in the square. Statues were shouting, police were shouting, granite blocks being torn up, heavy statues moving; the noise was becoming louder and louder, as everyone tried to make themselves heard over the din, and above it all, two police helicopters.

Then there came a new sound. A heavy pounding of footsteps that could only have come from a statue. With her hands on the stone balcony, Molly could feel vibrations coming up from street level. Who or whatever it was, was big.

It appeared in Cockspur Street to Molly's left. It was colossal. It was the statue of Achilles, and it looked invincible. It had come from Hyde Park, holding a shield on the left arm and a giant sword in the right hand. Its body ripped in well-defined muscle. Achilles waved the sword in the air high above his head, to the delight of the other statues, and the whole of Trafalgar Square erupted in cheering and shouting. The noise was deafening.

Molly felt vulnerable at the sight of the Achilles statue, even as high up as they were. This isn't right, she thought. Demonstrators come to Trafalgar Square to express their views, perhaps sometimes violently, but this is more than that. They're nearly all military men here. This looks like they're going to war."

"Charlie!" she shouted over the noise from below. "We've got to do something. We have to solve this."

Charlie looked at his sister.

"What do you mean, solve this?" said Gee-Gee, also having to shout.

"Come on, Charlie," said Molly. "Solve that clue. That's the answer, I know it is. Holmes wanted to tell me something and I think it is how to win this war. He knew this would happen, and he wanted to help us, that's why they've turned him back into a statue.

"You guessed it was an anagram?" continued Molly, encouraging her brother to concentrate. "You had words to do with the earth and heat but what else? Maybe we are thinking along the wrong path. Maybe it's not conservation."

"What anagram, what have I missed?" said Gee-Gee.

Molly remembered she hadn't seen Gee-Gee since before her capture, so he knew nothing about the message under Westminster Bridge.

"I went back to the Coade stone Lion, and climbed under the bridge. I found a message in paint from Sherlock Holmes."

"What did it say?" said Gee-Gee having to shout again.

Molly shouted back at him. "The Hearted Pirate."

The cheering stopped.

Everything stopped.

All the noise, the sounds and movement down below ceased. Completely and instantly, a silence fell upon Trafalgar Square.

Molly looked down over the balcony.

Every statue, stone or otherwise, was looking up at her. There was no mistake, Molly could feel their stare. It cut right into her. She tried to shrink back from the edge but couldn't move. She was petrified.

Molly heard Charlie make some sound but she was incapable of understanding what he was saying. She had never felt so exposed, so helpless. Some statues were moving forward, half a dozen maybe, towards the front of the building.

"We've got to get out of here," said Charlie as he placed his hands on Molly's shoulders and pulled her way from the balcony.

"Come on, Molly, now."

Molly looked at Gee-Gee for some explanation but he said nothing.

Charlie pushed his sister towards the balcony window, and Molly scrambled through, knocking papers and other articles from a desk. She robotically crossed the office and into the corridor transfixed in terror. They found the stairs and clattered their way downwards. Molly feared that her legs would give way, or that she would trip and fall. Her brother was already taking two steps at a time, and she was struggling to keep up. Before they got to the bottom, they could hear the sound of smashing glass and splintering wood. They slowed their descent being uncertain what they were running into. If they were to have any chance of escape, they had to get down before the statues got in.

At the bottom, Ochen was lying, face down on the floor. He wasn't moving. The first statue was still forcing its way through the remains of the front door, it seemed to be having trouble co-ordinating its feet and arms through the narrow opening.

Molly and Charlie stopped at the bottom of the stairs. All of a sudden, something occurred to Molly. If the first statue was just getting through the door, why was Ochen knocked out on the floor?

A male statue, dressed only in a toga, appeared from the corridor behind them. It was made of white stone that gave it an almost ghostly appearance. The toga resembled a stone, beach towel being clasped at the chest with one shoulder exposed as if the statue was naked underneath. To Molly, it looked malevolent. She screamed. She didn't mean to, it just came out.

Although the corridor was wide, the statue controlled it, and they now appeared to be trapped between the two attacking statues. They had to do something.

"Go for it, Molly," shouted Charlie and he pointed to the right hand side of the corridor as he ran to the left. He was already in front of Molly by the time she moved. The toga wearer moved to its right and swung out at Charlie with a clenched stone fist. Molly saw her chance and ran with a shoulder sliding along the corridor wall. She was passed and half way down the corridor when she turned to look for her brother. Charlie had been struck with a powerful stone arm and was sprawling down the corridor, arms outstretched, desperately trying to regain his balance. He impacted with the tiled floor.

For the second time, Molly screamed.

"Go, Molly, go," shouted Charlie who was now sprawled on the floor.

The toga-wearing statue turned towards Molly as if remembering who was the real goal. Molly ran; she had no choice. Down the corridor and through the door at the end. Left or right, both looked the same, she chose left, and through another door. This led to a row of offices and at the end of the corridor, a set of red-brown double doors. She ran to it, and smashed the small glass cylinder that housed the locking mechanism with the heel of her hand, and tumbled out onto the pavement.

Police, dressed in riot gear, were waiting for her. Having seen the statues smashing their way through the door and people on the balcony, they had deployed to the building. Molly ran to them and in a great burst of words, explaining that her brother was still inside. She had no idea about Gee-Gee or what he was doing.

The toga-wearing statue emerged, and scanned the scene for its victim. It spotted Molly and moved straight towards her. The police bravely stepped forward, waving long batons and striking the statue. It seemed a pointless exercise. The statue didn't flinch, it didn't deviate and it lashed out with a solid arm injuring police officers with every swing.

Molly pushed away from the police, knowing that they couldn't save her. She had to get away. She crossed Charing Cross Road looking for an exit, hesitant as her brother was still in there. There seemed to be fighting everywhere. Clusters of police with shields tackling individual statues; dogs barking, injured officers, some with obvious head injuries, sitting or crouched on the pavement being aided by colleagues or paramedics. A police car was on fire and two had been completely crushed. More sounds of guns being fired from the other side of the square, and she flinched with each shot. Smoke or gas, she wasn't sure which, drifted slowly across the road.

She hesitated, deciding what to do, then turned to see the toga statue was already right behind her. She sprinted into Northumberland Avenue, weaving between pieces of broken concrete and other debris, along with street signs, traffic lights, smashed barriers. She couldn't think about Charlie now, she had to get away.

It was menacing. It hadn't said anything. It hadn't explained why it was after her. It just kept on coming. The Hearted Pirate must have some significance and it must be threatening to the statues for them to react this way.

As Molly got to the end of Northumberland Avenue, she spotted a train coming across the river and into Charing Cross station. Getting on a train would be a good idea; surely, a statue's weight would prevent it from following and it would give her time to work on Holmes' clue. She sprinted up the road and took the steps into the station. The concourse was crowded. Molly didn't have time to join a queue, she started to push her way through. People complained, and she said sorry several times, but they had no appreciation of the danger she was in.

That was until Charles I appeared on horseback.

The statue, with curly hair and pointy beard, looked ridiculously small on a big horse. Even so, it was obvious he meant business as he spurred his steed. There was a clatter of hooves as the horse found the surface difficult. The crowd panicked and fled, many falling over each other to get away. Molly headed for the trains. She was instantly pursued by horse and statue.

Do something unexpected, Molly.

She jumped down off the platform between two waiting trains, and ran between them; her shoes crunched on the stones. There were shouts from railway staff but she ignored them. The gap between the trains was narrow, and she found herself running slightly sidewards. She didn't look behind her until she had more than cleared the last carriages of both trains; even then, she kept on going with a mixture of ungainly hops and skips because of the railway sleepers. The railway lines headed out across the river, all she had to do was keep going. She gave herself some advice about not touching any rails, as she had no idea if they were electric or not. This slowed her pace a little as she looked down to concentrate on where to put her feet.

It was the blaring of a loud horn that made her bring her head up, and she turned to see a train coming out of the station. She slowed to a fast walk checking that she wasn't on the same track as the departing train. She could clearly see the driver, who was standing up in his cab, staring at her while speaking into a radio.

If only you knew what I'm going through, she thought.

The train headed out across the river and she watched and waited for the carriages to pass so that she could check once more for any pursuers, statues or station staff. She could still hear a commotion coming from the platform. The tracks were empty, all the way from the station and up to — the ghostly white appearance of the toga-wearing statue came into view directly opposite. It had quickly moved up the track under the cover of the departing train. It stood staring at her, the toga wrapped around its naked body, there was no doubt, it meant her harm.

Molly felt desperate. She skipped over the tracks to the edge and looked over. There was one of the Golden Jubilee footbridges running closely alongside, and connected by long round poles and the suspension units. She looked down into the water, it wasn't welcoming. She couldn't possibly face another daring climb to safety. She was trapped and felt a growing panic.

The statue stepped over the tracks towards her. It appeared to be grinning. Molly wanted to reason with the statue. Why was it after her? What had she done? Then she thought about trying to outrun it, perhaps the statue wasn't that fit, or it might have to gather up all that material of its toga, giving Molly the chance to escape — on the other hand, it had kept pace with the departing train.

Another train blasted its horn, this time it was incoming and on the same track as Molly. Could things get any worse? The clunk-clunk of the carriages over the joints in the rail could be felt as a vibration through the bridge. By train standards, it wasn't going that fast but the driver didn't appear to be making any effort to stop. Molly stepped from between the rails to the edge. There wasn't much room. The statue stepped again. If she wasn't crushed by the train, she was going to be murdered by the statue. She bent down and picked up a handful of stones from between the sleepers. She also spotted an old metal pole, six feet long, black and oily lying on the ground.

The train blasted the air again with its deafening horn.

The statue stepped again. Molly lifted her right arm threw the handful of stones. The stones struck the statue in the face and scattered in all directions.

The statue stepped again.

Molly didn't wait to see how effective the stones had been, she was already picking up the metal pole. It was heavy and it stained her hands black. She lifted it behind her head using both hands.

"I'll smash you to a million pieces," she screamed, her face screwed up in fear and anger.

The statue, now standing between the tracks, reached out for her.

Molly swung the metal pole with everything she had. It whacked into the stone statue just at the shoulder, and a chunk of stone shot off across the tracks.

The statue showed no pain.

Molly's hands were stinging from the impact. She had just enough strength to draw the pole back and swing it again.

The statue caught it in mid-air with a powerful grip of its stone hand, and wrenched it from Molly's grip. That action sent her tripping forwards into the statue, and it grabbed hold of Molly by her denim jacket. It towered above her, its face and cold and menacing, and she knew it was going to kill her. Molly watched the metal pole as it was raised in an arc high above her head. This was it. A crushing blow from a weapon that she had provided. She had done her best but she could fight no more.

The train's horn blasted again, this time it was so close she felt the air vibrate with the sound. There was a screeching from metal on metal as the driver finally decided to brake.

Molly powered her legs to move, twisting herself out of her jacket at the same time. She spun, leapt over the tracks and away from the train. The statue, still holding Molly's empty jacket, looked puzzled as to how she had got away.

The impact was catastrophic as train hit statue. Molly cringed, and defensively protected her head with her arms. The statue spun as it was pushed up the track by the oncoming train; the train's wheels locked and couplings shunted. It was an horrible sight and sound, and she witnessed the look of shock in the driver's face. As the train shuddered to a stop, the statue catapulted forward, coming to rest between the tracks, ten feet from the front of the train.

Molly spotted police officers running up the track from the platforms. Cautiously, she stepped forward and walked towards the statue that was now lying in a rigid posture. It looked like a stone statue lying on its side, as if knocked off its plinth.

She stepped forward some more, timing her arrival at the statue's side with that of the police. Two of the police officers were armed and they pointed hand guns at the statue and warned Molly to stay back. Everyone stared at the statue. It was definitely solid, and no longer moving. A police officer gave it a prod with his boot. No one knew exactly what to do next.

"Does anyone know who the statue was?" said Molly.

The police shook their heads. He might look familiar but they couldn't place him.

"William Huskisson," said the train driver who had now climbed down from his train and was approaching the statue. "He was the MP for Liverpool in the seventeen, eighteen hundreds. He was also the first person to be killed by a train."

It was as though someone had just given Molly, next week's lottery numbers. "What did you say?" she asked the driver who was now looking at the damage to the front of his train.

"It was the famous Rocket train," he said, turning back to Molly, "he was attending the opening of the—"

"Quick," Molly shouted, interrupting the train driver's story. "Someone give me a pen and paper."

One of the police officers handed her is notebook and, in a circle, she scribbled down the letters.

T. H. E. H.E.A.R.T.E.D.P.I.R.A.T.E.

Her mind was racing. They can die. This statue died in the same manner as he had originally, by being struck by a train. She could see the word death and their. The final word emerged from her crossings out.

"Repeat! Repeat! Repeat their Death," she screamed out the words. "That's it!" Everyone looked at her.

"The Hearted Pirate is an anagram for Repeat their Death. That's the answer, that's how to defeat the statues." It seemed so obvious now that she'd solved it.

Molly explained everything to a police sergeant who then spent a long time talking on his phone. He was having trouble convincing his commanding officers that the whole solution to London's attack by statues, the threat of disease, water pollution and the collapse of infrastructure; had just been solved by a fifteen year old girl and an anagram.

At Molly's insistence, the police officer inquired as to the situation at Trafalgar Square, specifically about the whereabouts and welfare of her brother. When he finished he confirmed that her brother was safe, but they were still looking for Gee-Gee.

"There's no more time," said the statue of Winston Churchill, as he stood over the Prime Minister. "You are on the brink of a war for London. One person is dead and many are injured. That is regrettable. Soon this will develop into mass hysteria. You already have rioting on your streets. If I am forced to put our plan into action, tens of thousands will die in hours. There is no cure for this virus. You can stop all this, now, Prime Minister."

The Prime Minister sat with his head in hands. Somehow, Churchill's statue had found out about the calls to the SAS. The Prime Minister had also thought it a good idea to assemble some experts who knew about the strengths and weaknesses of stone and metal, to discuss the best way to destroy them. This group had met in secret.

Churchill had informed him that he was wasting his time.

This had all started out as a dream come true, our history coming to life. Now it was a nightmare.

Someone entered the Chamber and handed the Prime Minister a slip of folded paper.

"What does this mean?" said the Prime Minster, standing up quickly after reading it.

"Exactly what it says, sir. It's come from the police."

Churchill looked on.

The PM looked up at Churchill. "William Huskisson has been hit by a train at Charing Cross."

The Prime Minister waited for a response. There was none.

"That's how he died in real life. He is now lying on the tracks, as lifeless as stone."

Churchill's statue shifted position.

In Greek mythology, Achilles died when an arrow struck him in his heel, his one weakness. Lord Nelson was shot by a sniper. Charles I was beheaded, so was Sir Walter Raleigh. Richard the Lion Heart was hit by a crossbow arrow when he wasn't wearing his chainmail. Do you know, these are all things we could achieve again, today, right now."

Churchill coughed and cleared his throat.

"I'm sorry, did you have something to say?" said the Prime Minister stepping closer towards Churchill. "I can continue. Boudicca, currently raiding shops in Regent Street could be tricked into taking some poison. It was the natives of Hawaii who killed Captain Cook, with clubs and stones. We could probably even find some Hawaiians to do it for us."

The Prime Minister wasn't just showing off his knowledge of history, he was regaining control.

"Dear Abraham Lincoln was shot by John Wilkes Booth using a point four-four calibre Derringer. I'm sure we'll have one of those in a museum somewhere."

"Enough!" said Churchill.

"Precisely!" said the Prime Minister.

Thursday ...

The clear-up operation had gone through the night and into the early hours. It hadn't taken Churchill long to see that they were beaten. Their weakness had been found; he had no idea, at that stage, how. It also hadn't taken him long to stop the attack; there was no value in delaying. A quick mental communiqué to all statues had them sloping off to their respective plinths, bases, supports and platforms. There was no more fighting, no more violence, peace and calm fell over London once more.

There were too many statues to escort individually at the same time. The police were co-ordinating the movements. Some statues were allowed to go under their own steam, others were being loaded onto flat bed lorries and driven. All of these had motorcycle escorts. Under the threats from the statue of Churchill, the Prime Minister had complied with not bringing in the army, but that hadn't stopped him from having the military mobilise to the City limits, and they now rolled in with tanks, armoured vehicles, and an assortment of weaponry.

As each of the statues reached their usual place of residence, they settled back into their original pose, and simply lived no longer. There were no reports of statues saying a fond farewell or answering a last provocative question about history. Nor was there any last warning about saving the planet and the way forward. They simply turned to stone, or metal, or into whatever other material was used in their construction.

People on the street couldn't quite comprehend what was happening. Some sensed that it was all over ,and that this would be the last time they would see the statues in their living form. Some people cried, accepting now that they had missed a great opportunity. There was live Press coverage of all of this, of course.

The opposite also existed. People taunting the beaten statues as they walked along the city streets. Some statues were sprayed with paint or had derogatory signs hung on them. None of them retaliated. There was cheering and dancing, and some people suggested having street parties, reminiscent of the end of the World Wars.

Damage was wide spread. Statues weighing many tons had smashed paving slabs, gouged out tarmac roads and fractured sewers, gas and water pipes. There was damage to vehicles, shop windows and buildings, not forgetting the destruction caused by opportunists joining the cause and having nothing to do with the statues. The cost would be in the millions, if not billions.

Aside from the physical and financial damage caused over the last few days, there would be a scar left on London and its people visible to the whole world. What was to be done with the statues now? Will they ever try this again? What about conservation and their message? What effect will this have on the people that had contact with the statues?

With surprising ease, the statue of Sir Winston Churchill clambered back up onto his plinth in the Members' Lobby. He shuffled his feet around as if looking for the exact spot. Standing below him was the Prime Minister, Home Secretary and several of the Cabinet members. The Prime Minster looked as if he was saying goodbye to an unwelcome relative, who had called unexpectedly, and perhaps that's exactly how he felt. In truth though, with time to reflect on the whole affair, he would regret not making more of this moment with the statue of Sir Winston Churchill.

"Now, don't let the people over-react and start pulling statues down or putting them in wooden boxes," said Churchill's statue. "It's just not necessary. You have beaten us fair and square, and we have all gone back to our rightful places. All statues have returned, including the two royal marines." Churchill shook his head. "Lord only knows where they've been. There's no threat to London's water, we didn't get round to releasing any deadly virus, and we've not left anything horrible lurking behind."

"Was there a deadly virus?" said the Prime Minister.

"We came here to bring you a message," said Churchill. "About the planet and how it is being abused. There's no quick fix but equally there's no necessity to keep on talking about it. You've done enough debating, get on and act, and make those actions count. Work together. Remember, we shall be watching."

The statue of Churchill assumed its normal position, hands on hips, jacket pushed back, left leg forward. A slight rotundity to his belly making him look more solid. He then turned to lifeless bronze.

There was a universal sigh of relief, and ministers started shaking hands with each other in congratulations.

"And another thing!" Churchill shouted. "Leave my damn shoe alone, it looks bloody odd with it being a different colour."

He had spoken for the last time.

As daylight was appearing on the skyline, Molly climbed into the back of the police car. She wanted to say, 'home James, and don't spare the horses,' as allegedly said by Queen Victoria, but didn't think the officers would appreciate it. Her entire body ached and she was well past the point of being hungry.

It had been the maddest three days of her life. She'd warned people that things weren't right, and proved it. Risked her life, more than once, and then come up with the solution that had saved London. Madness — who would have thought?

She had provided what details she had on the Agalmata, to the police; it wasn't much. Gee-Gee, it seemed, had gone into hiding. She explained how she had worked out the clue, which had led to the statues' defeat. The police had asked her to make a statement and there was talk that she would be invited to meet the Prime Minister, maybe even the Queen. It was also explained to her that her story would eventually come out, and she would get a lot of interest from the media. The police officer had frowned at that point, and said she should speak to her parents before saying anything to the Press.

She still hadn't made contact with her brother who had been taken to hospital, treated and discharged, and the police had kindly driven him home, and conveyed his whereabouts to Molly over their radio.

The police car turned up Portland Place and into the Marylebone Road. Trafalgar Square area was still closed off. Molly had a thought.

"Could you please take me to Baker Street station," she said.

"Sure," said the driver. "Anything in particular?"

"Yes, I want to say thanks to a good friend."

The police car turned left and pulled up outside Baker Street station. Molly got out of the car and walked up to the statue of Sherlock Holmes. He stands on a polished granite plinth, holding his pipe in his right hand, one shoe is just off the edge of the plinth as if he is about to step down.

Molly put her hand over the shoe and looked up into his face. Why had he helped her? She smiled at the statue, willing him to give some sign or gesture. He remained motionless.

"Thank you," she said. "I couldn't have done it without you."

Molly put her key in the door, then turned and waved goodbye to the police officers. The door opened before she could turn the key, and there was her brother with an arm in a sling and some cuts to his face. They hugged as best they could then Molly closed the door behind her.

"A cup of tea is what we need," said Charlie.

"No thanks," she said, following her brother into the kitchen, "I'm done with drinking tea. Tell me what happened to you after I ran out the building."

Charlie and Molly swapped stories, both equally enthralled by what had happened to each other, and relieved that they had both come out of the ordeal, alive.

"Repeat their death, of course," said Charlie clicking his fingers. "I think I would have got it in the end."

Molly smiled. "What about Amber, shouldn't you call her?"

"Yeah, maybe, I was thinking, she's not really for me. What about Gee-Gee?"

"Umm, I just don't know. I think if we ever see him again, he's got some more explaining to do," she said.

"Will you speak to Mum and Dad about the Agalmata and what Gee-Gee told us?" said Charlie.

"Yes, we have to. I want to know why we've never been told about me being sick, and who was the Mayan man who made me better? I also want to know how the statues knew so much about me."

Molly was more than tired, she was completely drained and in need of sleep, but at the same time she sensed something else. It was as though she wanted the adventure to continue, perhaps with a little less fear and danger. She did need a bath, and to treat her cuts and bruises, and then she could do with talking with Mum and Dad.

She looked over to the phone.

As if on cue, the telephone rang. Molly picked it up.

"Mum! Where are you? Heathrow? Oh, my God, are you OK? Is Dad with you? Mum, Dad, you won't believe what's been happening here, me and Charlie got kidnapped by statues and they wanted to take over and ..." Molly poured it out in one long sentence.

"Calm down, Molly," said her mother.

Her mother explained that they had actually seen the statues of Alcock and Brown from the plane as they were taking off. They had dismissed it as not real, and not thought about it until they read it in the papers. They tried ringing but couldn't get an answer and then caught the next available flight home.

"We're getting a cab from here, be with you very soon," said her mother.

Molly put the phone down.

"Great," said Charlie. "Mum and Dad are back. We've a lot to tell them."

"And they've a lot to tell us," said Molly.

"Do you think all the statues will be pulled down, at least in London?" said Charlie.

Molly thought about Sherlock Holmes being pulled down and destroyed.

"I don't think they should," she said. "I think they should be left as a reminder. Not how great people have been, but how human they were. We should remember they had good bits and bad bits. They did the best they could. We shouldn't put them on a plinth or pedestal, or look at them in such grandeur. We should understand them for who they were. Do you remember what I told you about how Gee-Gee explained what Agalmata meant?" Molly continued. "The Greeks held their statues in such high esteem, believing them to have special powers that they made them into Gods. Maybe we do the same?"

"I suppose they wanted to live as much as we do," said Charlie.

"Edith Cavell said to me that they wanted to survive," said Molly. "Was that an existence with us, or without us, who knows?"

Molly considered for moment, just how different things would have been if the statues hadn't been defeated.

"I couldn't have done it without your help, you know," she said, looking across at her brother.

"Me? I didn't do anything, it was you, Molly, the fame is all yours. You were right all along about the statues."

Molly sighed. "I don't want fame. I'm pleased I've been able to do something worthwhile, but I don't think I was completely right. I believed they were planning something other than their conservation message. Why, I don't know. Gee-Gee once said that I'd been frightened by one and embarrassed by another, and as you have pointed out, I just don't like statues. When I was writing a statement for the police, someone from the government came to see me; to say thanks, I suppose. He told me the statues had threatened to release a smallpox virus but they hadn't done so. It would have killed a lot of people. The government man said that so far, they hadn't found any trace of any virus. I don't know if the statues were really trying to take over, or if they wanted us to think they were, so that we would act on their message."

"How do you mean?"

"Think about it. Even with something as amazing as living, breathing statues, were we ever going to do something about the plight of the world? They had to wage war to really get our attention. To convince us that they could and would take over."

Charlie nodded. "I guess if the statues had really wanted to take over, they could have all come alive? Not just London but all over the world?"

"And why did they give in at the end. Repeat their death doesn't work for all statues. Some of them died of natural causes."

"Do you think something else is going to happen?"

Molly shrugged. "I think we'll have to wait and see.

Epilogue ...

The telephone next to his bed was ringing. The Prime Minister rolled onto his left side and reached out. He glanced at the bedside clock — four thirty in the morning.

A voice spoke to him, "Sorry to wake you Prime Minister. You have an urgent call from the President of the United States. He is telephoning on a secure line from America."

The President of the United States came on the line in his easily recognisable accent. He sounded agitated, maybe even a little scared.

"Mr Prime Minister?" he said. "Prime Minister, you've got to help me. The Statue of Liberty is missing. It's as though she's just walked off."

THE END

Printed in Great Britain
by Amazon